PRAISE FOR CATHERINE FORDE:

Tug of War

- 'Another gripping story . . . good stuff from an author who never disappoints' – *Independent*
- 'Skilfully observed and rich in its emotional depth' – *Achuka*
- 'A raw and perceptive story' – *Books for Keeps*
- 'Delicious' – *Sunday Telegraph*

Firestarter

- 'A gripping and edgy thriller that keeps the reader on the edge of their seat' – *Bookseller*
- 'A powerful thriller' – *Publishing News*
- 'Penetrating and powerful . . . (Forde) is amongst the best of today's writers for teenagers' – *Sunday Herald* (Glasgow)
- 'Catherine Forde's novels have the emotional impact of a clenched fist to the stomach. She writes powerful prose that deliver firm blows' – *Achuka*

The Drowning Pond

- 'Bitingly plausible, this is a gripping page-turner' – *Guardian*

- 'Expertly crafted, with characters full of bite and vitality' – *Glasgow Herald*

Skarrs

- 'A novel that is both troubling and inspirational' – *Guardian*
- 'A heady mix of broken glass emotions, tough, edgy dialogue and page-turning storytelling' – *Publishing News*
- 'One of the best children's books I've ever read. It's raw, poetic, beautifully written, and frighteningly real.' – Kevin Brooks
- 'A gripping read, which you can't put down' – *Yorkshire Post*

Fat Boy Swim

- 'Fat Boy Swim should be force-fed to every secondary school child' – *Sunday Telegraph*
- 'Powerful, empowering and often very funny' – *The Times*
- 'A moving, tumultuous, roller-coaster, acid-etched story' – *Bookseller*
- 'Moving, shocking but thoroughly engrossing . . . A powerful book' – *Carousel*

Hey Jess,
Enjoy!

sugarcoated

Catherine FORDE

WARNING:
contains violence

EGMONT

Also by Catherine Forde:

Exit Oz
Fat Boy Swim
Firestarter
I See You Baby . . .
(with Kevin Brooks)
L-L-L-LOSER
Skarrs
The Drowning Pond
The Finding
Think Me Back
Tug of War

For Pauline

EGMONT

We bring stories to life

First published in Great Britain 2008
by Egmont UK Limited
239 Kensington High Street
London W8 6SA

ISBN 978 1 4052 2931 9

1 3 5 7 9 10 8 6 4 2

www.egmont.co.uk
www.catherineforde.co.uk

A CIP catalogue record for this title is available from the British Library

Typeset by Avon DataSet Ltd, Bidford on Avon, Warwickshire
Printed and bound in Great Britain by the CPI Group

contents

part 1

crumblies ahoy!

There I was, slumped over Dad's appointment book. Doodling speccy faces to match the names in it. Trying not to die of boredom. Thinking nothing *ever* happens round here . . .

Next thing, four palms thudded flat against Dad's shop window. The racket jerked me so rigid the castors of my chair shot from under me. I landed on my backside behind the reception desk, legs in the air. OK. Soft landing. But hardly a flattering pose for a Big Girl. By the time I scrabbled upright the same four palms were splutting along the glass. Leaving smeary pawprints.

'Crumblies Ahoy,' I hissed; although to anyone looking in, my eyes were crinkled into crescents of joy. My expression was totally phoney, though. Forced. Because Dad insisted patients must be greeted with a friendly face.

'Go away,' I waved out at these two cotton tops,

who were now peering in at me through circles they'd made for their eyes with their thumbs and index fingers. To watch me smiley-smiling, you'd think seeing old Mr and Mrs Mullen had made my day. Would never guess I was growling through my grin, 'Just shuffle off and die you ancient –'

'Yoo hoo, hen,' Mrs Mullen's quaver misted Dad's glass. 'Where's the opticians? Canny see it.'

I showed all my teeth.

'Can you see *this*?' I flicked the Mullens a vicky with the KitKat I'd be guzzling as soon as my dad toddled himself off for lunch.

'Oi, behave yourself, Clod,' Dad said to me.

Shucking off the sad white coat he felt he needed to wear for staring into milky cataracts all day, Dad put himself between my scowl and his shop window. He kept his voice low. Finger a-wagging.

'Let the old souls have their joke and keep smiling out till they bugger off,' he told me. 'Then clean my window. All *righty*!' Putting on his professional smile and his outdoor jacket, Dad twitched the Mullens a palsy-walsy wink.

'Mum leaves glass-wipes under the till,' he instructed me with the same cheesy smile. 'Make sure you lock the shop while you're out cleaning. And no playing with my phones or breaking my computer. See you at two.'

As he spoke, Dad was flinging the door open, his tone morphing from Claudia Quinn's Bossy Pa to Mr Friendly Local Optician.

'Well LOOK who's here again! Always a sight for sore eyes. Get it? Sight? Sore eyes? Going my way?' he boomed at the Mullens, steering them well clear of his shop. They were too busy beaming back at him to notice his pernickety head-jerk from me to the dirty window: *Get cleaning, Clod!*

'Yeah. **See** you, Pa. Get it?'

Before Dad was out of sight, I'd two KitKat fingers rammed into my mouth whole.

Didn't a gal deserve *some* pleasure?

'Working here all sodding Saturday for twenty-five quid,' I chewed. Where Dad found patience to deal with doddery gits like the Mullens I DID NOT KNOW. And my mum? She was even better. *Always* charming managing Dad's practice and his brigade of blindos for more than twenty-five years. Grace itself.

'By name and by nature,' as Dad liked to wag about Mum. Always up for a bit of banter, she was. Always ready with a tasteful joke . . .

Unlike me: Grace and Sean's Utter Lost Cause Of A Daughter. Who frankly, could not be *assed* trying to be civil to folk so past it they didn't even bother to switch their hearing aids on, let alone put in their false teeth.

'Frigging twilight zone this place, so it is,' I was muttering while I scuffed out the shop with glass-wipes in one hand and a second KitKat poking out my mouth. Naturally, I didn't bother locking up like Dad warned. Get real.

It wasn't like some joker was going to make off with the till in the next thirty seconds. Not when the handprints I was wiping away counted as High Drama in Greenwood Shopping Centre.

Deadsville, I scowled at my freshly gleaming reflection. Beyond myself I could see Dad stepping out in front of this big black off-road car thing. You know the kind yummy-mummies like to park on zigzags?

D'you call it an SOB or STD or SUV . . . *I* don't know, do I?

Whatever, Dad made it brake hard so the Mullens could shuffle across the shopping centre car park at zero miles an hour. Dad, like he was their personal lollipop man, stayed with the Mullens till they reached the pavement. Whenever they said something, Dad threw his head back and roared and laughed. You'd think he was enjoying a private audience with Billy Connolly, instead of tolerating a couple of oldies drabber than their tartan shopping trolley, whose idea of hilarity was groping up to the window of Quinn's Eyecare with their even drabber joke:

'Help. I've lost my guide-dog.'

For a change it wasn't crumblies who mucked my Mr Sheeny window next. It was 'yooths' as the Mullens would say. And what's really galling is that while I was out wiping off traces of the Mullens' pawprints I *thought* I heard sniggering nearby. A voice snorting, 'Check the state of that big lassie's muffin top, man!'

Being stupid, it didn't cross my mind that *moi* could

possibly be the source of mirth wafting from this trio whose white tracksuits glowed in the shadows of Gluehead Alley along from our shop.

Stoners, I decided. Crackheads.

Wrong.

No sooner was I back behind reception tucking into a sultana scone than the white tracksuits lined up outside. I assumed they were showing off their combined mathematical skills to each other when they counted to three in turn. But then they gobbed. Smeared their tags in the dribbles:

Big Eck. Rotty. Blotto.

And skedaddled.

As I belted out with the wipes again, taking a few token steps in pursuit then stopping to hurl a fruity mouthful of abuse instead – 'Ya shower of trolls!' – one of Dad's more intrepid narcotic-dependent patients seized his moment.

Six Armani frames for sale in the *entire* shop. This waster trousered them all.

Dad would dock my wages for that one. To teach me a lesson: *'What d'I tell you about leaving the practice unattended, Clod? Can't you pay attention to one simple instruction?'*

Man, I was totally *seething* while I dabbed the window this second time. Manky it was. Never mind giving ASBOs to the white tracksuits. With phlegm that colour, at least two of them needed antibiotics.

'Crap day. Only half over,' I complained while I disinfected my hands in Dad's back shop. Outside someone was trying the door.

'Locked. Saturday. Ridiculous!' A woman's voice exclaimed. 'Mr Quinn's lassie phoned to say my specs were in. Never said Mr Quinn shut for lunch.'

'Just scram, missus,' I sniggered into the mirror at the round-faced ginger girl with a set of shop-keys between her teeth.

I took my time – brushing my hair, checking for dandruff, dealing with a couple of blackheads – before I slipped back behind reception. Coast was clear outside. I'd peace to finish my scone.

'Take five,' I chuckled, keeping hunkered down, head tucked below the desk so the shop would look deserted to passing trade.

As a thick layer of butter yielded to my teeth I dislodged a cluster of sultanas. Before they hit the floor I dived to save them.

And for the third time that morning Dad's window was walloped.

2

through the glass

This time though, the glass was scudded with so much force that the fluorescent kiddie frames I'd taken half an hour of my life to stack into an artful pyramid, tumbled from their display.

'Piss off,' I tutted, edging on hands and knees to peek round the desk and check the state of the window. 'You'll crack m'dad's glass, hitting it like tha–' I was ready to pull myself upright. March outside. Give someone a bit of grief.

Then I froze.

A hand – Massive. Splayed. – was pressed to the window. Must have been leaning hard. Really hard. I could tell because both the fleshy base of the thumb and the fingertips were white. Almost fluorescent. Totally bled of colour. Especially in contrast to the dense gout of blood they were streaking as the hand slid down the glass. Slow-motion slow.

'Oi –'

That was the extent of my protest. My voice a bleat. That's if I even spoke aloud. No idea.

Such a rammy outside.

Ten feet away.

Telly screen distance.

Maybe less.

And so much blood.

Slapped on the window like paint.

Then so much violence.

Real.

A layer of glass from me.

Thank Christ I'd locked the door.

Because the next thing to hit the window was a man's head.

Full force it glanced the glass. Temple first. I watched long grey hair stranding the thick blood-splat. Pooling it wider. But only for the length of a blink. No sooner did I register that the muffled crack I'd heard was human skull-bone meeting something rigid – horrible, horrible, *horrible* sound – than two ringed hands gripped the head by the hairline. Yanked it back.

Then slammed it even harder against the window. This time the impact dispersed blood like a gory sunburst. Only the centre of the window stayed unspattered. That's where the man's head . . .

Would you listen to me? I nearly said *rested*. But only his eyeball made contact with the glass. It was mashed against it. Staring full open. Fishy. Unblinking. Fixed on the middle distance. Pupil downturned. Towards the floor. Staring. Right where I cowered.

Staring back.

Unblinking.

We were eyeball to eyeball.

'But he can't see me. He won't see me,' my throat gurgled. Dry and strangled-sounding through my open mouth. Scone mulch was clogging the back of my tongue. But I didn't dare swallow. Daren't move.

Crouched behind the desk, I prayed the eye still holding my gaze couldn't really see me. Prayed that whoever I could hear whispering through the glass, 'Help, please,' wasn't talking to me.

Because two different eyes – heavy lidded, monobrow-shadowed – were at the window now.

And a black-gloved fist was swiping the glass clear of blood so the new eyes could scan the shop.

'Some bastard watching.' Black Glove's voice was a growl with a foreign accent. His words a threat; not a question.

'No. Shop shut. Keep going.' A different voice replied. Staccato. Also foreigny. But the hammer in the gloved hand rapped the window all the same.

Lightly.

Playfully almost, as a matching gloved hand lent shade to the eyes sweeping the shop. They narrowed on Dad's vacant waiting area, darting from the reception desk to the blind racks of frames stretching one wall. Back to the desk. But they didn't see me. Sure they didn't see me. *Coz I'm low down. Hidden. Not moving.* I allowed myself a gulp of air. And then the hammer swung back from the glass.

Oh not Dad's window. That was my first thought.

Don't ask what my second one was. I don't remember. Because I've never exactly seen, at close range, a man hit with a hammer.

Have you?

Across the back of the skull.

Then on the neck.

Then full in the face.

That first blow splatted the victim against the window. Wumph! Chest striking first, followed by hands. Nose. Forehead. Chin. The second crack drove his mouth against the glass. *Jeez Louise,* I really hope the way this man's eyes rolled up meant he was unconscious already, because when his full weight stonked the window, his teeth smashed against it.

And I mean *smashed.*

When he slid towards the ground his upper lip peeled away from his gums. He looked as if he was grinning at me through his own blood and saliva and broken teeth.

'See this. And *this*. And *this*.'

Three more times – Calm. Rhythmic. Like it really knew what it was doing – the black glove rose to pound at this man now slumped outside. He wasn't moving.

'This. This. This.' The second foreigny voice repeated. Its accent was precise. Its tone, more excited than his accomplice's, rose with each word. Practically squealing this other man was, as he bounced on tiptoes round the victim, light footed as a bantam weight. Filled the measured intervals between each hammer blow with a vicious, random kick.

Thigh. Groin. Side. Ribs.

Somehow, what he, the dancing man was doing, seemed worse to me than the hammering. His contact more personal.

Stop it. Stop it. Stop it. I heard myself chant but I don't know whether my voice or my head was speaking. My body was petrified. Literally.

Otherwise I'd have shut my eyes or covered my face with my hands or fast-forwarded or changed over or switched off or flicked to teletext or turned away like I do whenever a violent scene begins on telly.

But here I was: stone.

And I witnessed *everything*.

Wasn't over yet, either.

Before the attackers disappeared down Gluehead Alley, they heaved their victim away from the window. At least, they tried to, but he must have been too heavy for them to move, so they gave up. Flung him down in a crumple across the wheelchair ramp outside Dad's shop. Used their heels to roll him on to his back, heedless when the dead weight of his head lolled behind his torso and cracked off the concrete. They straightened his legs. Spread his arms wide at his side. Smoothed his fingers out. It was all very, very matter of fact.

Then Black Glove straddled him.

'See this, dog?' I heard him say, heavy accent almost pleasant. He raised the hammer over his head with both hands. Gave his accomplice a nod.

'Hands off. Boss says.'

As the foreigny voice hissed, Black Glove drove his weapon into the left hand of the man beneath him. His full weight coming down with it. When Black Glove raised the hammer again, I managed to force my eyes shut. Didn't watch the hammer fall. Heard it land, though. Won't ever forget the sound.

'Yes, hands off.'

This time Black Glove gave the warning.

When I opened my eyes, both attackers were gone.

3

questions, questions...

'So who phoned the police?'

'Ambulance?'

'Went out to see if the bloke on the ground was alive?'

Questions. Questions. Nothing *but* in the couple of hours after the attack. Most of them bouncing back and forth outside Dad's shop. That's where an arthritic semi-circle gathered to mutter round the mound of unconscious man. Remained long after he was bagged and splinted and stretchered and sirened to hospital. This sounds sick, given what had just happened, but there was a real upbeat vibe to these rubberneckers. Pensioners the lot of them. From inside the shop I heard them shouting into each other's hearing aids, cheerily post-morteming what had just happened.

Or what they *thought* had just happened:

'That fella on the ground had a gun in each hand, did you see?'

No. There was no gun.

'And what about that blade yon skinny bloke flashed?'

What blade?

'Serrated, wasn't it?'

That man was attacked by a hammer.

'Aye, giant teeth on it.'

Bollocks.

'Fishing knife, maybe?'

Get yourself in here for an eye test.

'And the bloke with the hammer? A blackie, wasn't he?'

You colour blind now? He was white. Same as the other fella. One thickset and dark, wearing black gloves, the other slight and fair. Chav rings on all his fingers. I saw both men, remember? I witnessed everything.

For the usual clientele of Greenwood Shopping Centre, two thugs hammering lumps out of someone else was a *major* novelty. Not only did it provide fresh blood for entertainment instead of fake telly gore, but, even better, Scene of Crime Officers who weren't actors in real life kept piling out of vans, stepping into noddy suits, and swarming about the place. Sure beat your full Sky package on the box!

Normally round here, apart from truants pilfering Kwiksave, the odd car window being panned, and occasional junkies knocking Dad's stock to sell in the pub for a ten quid wrap of temporary happiness, crimes were mainly committed when the shops were shuttered. All my dad's patients safe in their high-rises watching murders on *C.S.I.* That was when the dodgem-like opening hours chaos of Greenwood's car park morphed from crammed to tumbleweed deserted. Then the area became a no-go zone; its traffic-free concourse an arena for Buckfast-fuelled stand-offs between local teenage gangs, its doorways the business premises of dealers and their clients.

So the nosey parkers clucking outside Dad's window belonged to a parallel world. That was why the leaking of *proper* violence into it was as alien and exciting as a spaceship outside Somerfield.

'Ooooh, police are in there now? See. Did Mr Quinn's big lassie call the cops?'

'Wonder if she put that fella in the recovery position?'

'He was choking on his tongue, face was turning blue –'

'If she did she's sharper than she looks, eh?'

Inside Dad's shop there was a bit more decorum. That's why I could hear everything being said outside. None of it correct, by the way.

Not, I'd already decided, that I planned to put anyone straight on The Facts. I might be the big daft lassie that Mr Double-Vision Dobson with chronic diabetes was still pointing and shaking his head at, but I'm not *completely* stupid.

Come on? After witnessing how heavy-eyed Black Glove and his sidekick warned people off, do you think I'd *volunteer* to create their photofits on some police computer? I wanted to hang on to *my* smile, at least till the price of laser whitening dropped.

So. Er. No. Safer to do a three wise monkeys while I faced the official version of the questions being posed outside:

'Did *you* report this? Are you a witness?'

That was Dad. First person to question me. This was

after he barged through the crowd of patients clutching his arm for information.

'Oh Mr Quinn. We're that worried you were . . .'

He ignored the blue and white police tape across his doorway, giving its authority the respect due a cobweb when he tore it down.

'Behave yourself, sonny. My daughter's in there,' I heard him interrupt the squat cop manning Quinn's entrance like it was a goal mouth.

'Sir, you're trespassing –' the cop warned.

'On my own property, Rambo? Aye right!' Dad snorted. 'Where are you, Cloddy?'

He found me in the back kitchen. Came straight to me. His hand cupped my cheek, eyes probing mine like when he tested them. Looking for problems: *What have you seen?*

Before I could tell Dad anything – or nothing – two uniformed cops banged in with their own questions. One doing the talking. Other licking his biro.

'So *was* it you who called this in, er . . . Claudia?'

'And did you leave the shop to check that the man was alive?'

'Did you, Cloddy?' This was Dad again. *Round here? You nuts?* his tone implied.

Finally, I was grilled by detectives. Pair of them showed up. Grey suits. Stale, instant-coffee breath. Bellies. Bad skin. Both of them had the same flat seen-it, done-it, bought-the-T-shirt voices.

'So. You saw what happened? Requested the emergency services?' the first detective tried to put words into my mouth. DCI Stark, his badge read.

'No. Didn't need to,' I replied. 'Ambulance came right away.'

'You didn't summon assistance?'

This second detective's badge was smaller: DI Hatch. *Starsky and Hutch,* I thought as soon as I read those names. *Surely a joke?* I'd to choke back the giggles while I was busy telling them, 'No. I said already. Called no one. Didn't need to.'

'Were you the first to attend the victim?'

'No. Ambulance came right away. No point in me interfering.'

'So *what did* you see exactly –?'

'– Just describe any small detail of the attack.'

The detectives' questions overlapped. Just like they do on telly interrogations when they're tightening the screws on a suspect or a stroppy witness. So just like an uncooperative character on one of my cop shows, I shrugged all the time they were talking.

'Just give us anything you witnessed –'

'– description of the attackers. Weapon –'

'– anything you heard –'

'– that could identify –'

'Nothing.' I cut in as soon as I could. 'Window was belted. I hid behind the desk. Heard shouting. Didn't look –' I was shaking my head.

'Yes, but tell –'

'– us *anything* you –'

'– saw or –'

'– heard. Anything at –'

'– all, Claudia –'

It didn't matter how often I told Starsky and Hutch: 'I saw nothing. Heard nothing,' they repeated the same questions. Even when I grew upset.

Turned dizzy. Had to lean over the sink in the shop kitchen.

'What *did* you see?'

'Hear?'

'Must have witnessed *something*.'

The detectives kept quizzing me, even while I was dry heaving, a policewoman taller than myself and called Marjory holding back my hair and pressing wet paper towels to my forehead. Dad's arm was round my waist, too. When I threatened to barf for real they both interrupted the detectives:

'Right. That's enough with my daughter for now.'

'Boss, she's had a helluva fright. Could we lay off.'

Marjory's voice was deeper than Dad's, and I was impressed with her effect on her DCI. When she thrust out her chest – not in a sexy way, in case you're wondering – both DI and DCI pocketed their notebooks.

Turned out this was nothing to do with her though.

'Sorry, Marge. Would you listen to us? Getting all carried away like we're the real –'

'Starsky and Hutch, boss. But you're not. And we're in Glasgow, not California –'

When Marjory interrupted her superiors I'd to jackknife over the sink. Run the tap and splash my face to camouflage a guffaw I couldn't silence. Her deadpan putdown exposed what could only be Stark and Hatch's hilarious fantasy: *These old guys secretly see themselves running about in a Ford Torino, solving crimes. How sad is that . . .* I snorted under the running water till Starsky-Stark tapped my hip with his mobile.

'We're about through here for now. Just asking you as much as we can to –'

'– save us all a return visit. You've been a help, Claudia.'

When I turned, Hutch-Hatch was yawning and stretching.

'Ay, ay, ay. Long shift. We'll be off. Wagons roll, lads! Head for the hills.' Hutch-Hatch swept his arm towards the dozen or so uniformed cops who must have multiplied inside Dad's shop while I was hanging over the sink. When I saw how much they were enjoying themselves while on duty, I couldn't help thinking that maybe a job with the police would be the ideal ticket for a girl like me who didn't like to gee herself, wasn't too flush in the brain-cell department, and enjoyed a bit of a laugh. The uniforms were certainly having that, modelling Dad's *Extraordinarily Cheap'n'Nasty* range of two-tone tinted bingo glasses, wearing them squinty or upside down, and jostling for shots at a mirror. Three or four laughing policemen – hotties all, or maybe it was just the uniforms blinding me to their individual shortcomings – were literally reduced to tears of mirth.

Note to self, I mentally jotted. *Pop into Careers ASAP for info on minimum entry requirements to Strathclyde Plodsworth.*

'Nice big place, this, Mr Q, isn't it? Good range of stock, haven't you? Been here long? Mind if I look round?'

So the DCI wasn't leaving yet after all. While I was still congratulating myself on coming up with a career pathway that might just make it easier for my dad to accept his only daughter was never going to produce enough grey matter to keep the name of Quinn Family Eyecare alive, I heard Starsky-Stark – still asking questions.

'Coming up thirty years.'

Dad sounded distracted answering the detective. He kept checking over his shoulder like he didn't want to leave me alone in the back-shop with Marjory. I didn't want him to leave me either. Her kindness was scaring me. When I followed him through the shop my legs were blancmange.

Cellulite inside as well as outside.

'Everyone done here now? Can I get on with running my business?' Dad opened his shop door and windmilled his arm in a gesture that said 'Leave' to the cops inside. But all that happened was the chatter from the gathered gore-seekers outside billowed into the shop too.

Only DI Hutch-Hatch took the hint.

'Right. Show's over folks. Howz about you vamoose? Less any of you feel like giving statements. Down the station.' I noticed how he barely raised his voice and the crowd zimmered and hobbled and limped away. *There* was authority!

Meanwhile, inside the shop, the DCI was still putting questions to Dad. 'Thirty years you're here?

Would you credit it?' He seemed in no hurry to leave.

'Must be needing new gregs, don't you think? D'you know this is the first time I've noticed an optician's here? Boom. Boom. Eh? Eh?'

He illustrated his own joke-cum-question, lurching and groping round in a circle. Like Dad had *never* heard that one before.

'And you just recently promoted for your astonishing powers of observation, sir?'

This was Marjory, deadpan, passing me to join her colleagues. She left my shoulder stinging from her farewell slap.

'Funny thing is, it's not like I'm never down this patch, you know? Mainly after hours, mind you. Got a business card, Mr Quinn?' DCI Starsky-Stark was quizzing Dad, handing his own card over. 'My next day off I'll come in with the wife, will I? After all she'll be the one looking at me in my specs, eh?'

The detective's wink, as he joined his partner in the doorway, was for my benefit.

Then, like a freeze-frame at the end of a scene in some cheesy cop show, Starsky-Stark and Hutch-Hatch turned to have the last word.

'Mind you,' the DCI told his partner, 'we'll be back sooner if the joker who's dirtied Mr Quinn's window croaks it, won't we now –'

'Roger that. We'll have one less bad guy to chase,' the DI replied in his flat, on-duty voice again, 'but another bloody mess to mop up.'

The detectives were outside Dad's shop. Both lighting fags from the same match. Mooching to their car with hunched shoulders.

'Drug turf war, this carry-on. Organised crime. Nasty people,' Marjory shrugged. 'Though we'll probably only bother you folks again if carnations and teddy bears start piling up out here. Happens soon as someone dies these days. Should've been a florist, me, in a city like this,' she said, downturning her mouth at the slick of congealing blood she nearly stepped in with her big plod-cop shoes.

sweet-talking guy

'Less than an hour I leave you and it's Gangsta's Paradise in Greenwood. Just as well your mum's Down Under.'

My dad was sighing at his window. You could hardly see out it. Patches of the glass were rose tinted, where the dried bloodstains were thin. Others were daubed with rusty brown slicks, thick enough to cut the light coming through. As if the shop wasn't dim enough, every inch of the window was aluminium-powder dusted for fingerprints. No wonder there hadn't been a customer through the door since the attack. I mean, for an OAP with angina, stepping over the chalked outline of a whacked man to get your eyes tested was kinda offputting.

'And they tell me they're sending more forensics before I can clean up and get back to normal.'

Dad stopped kneading his love handles and

glowering at the police photographer to sort all the scattered frames the cops had played with. A no-brain-strain-job like that was normally my responsibility but since Starsky and Hutch had left with Marjory, I wasn't worth a button. Once I'd phoned to confuse all Dad's afternoon appointments by telling them, 'Hello. I'm calling from Quinn's the optician's. We're not here today,' I was done in. Just sat behind reception, staring through the stained glass window, my hand going automatically from my mouth to the box of Brazil nuts some satisfied patient had left Mum about two years ago. I wired in till both trays were empty. What a porker! I don't even like Brazil nuts. Even fresh ones. Does anyone? They stink your breath. I was humming too. Songs from *The Lion King*. Through my nose. I like humming. Always calms me down. Don't understand why it winds other people up so much. I mean, humming absently through your nose is hardly as heinous as the way people absently *pick* theirs. Then eat their excavations.

Anyway, apart from the highest bits of *Circle of*

Life, I wasn't humming *that* out of tune. Well, *I* didn't think so.

Still, it wound Dad up something else.

'Cloddy, for the love of God,' he interrupted just as I was drawing a deep breath to do justice to the chorus of *Can You Feel the Love Tonight?* 'Take your wages out the till. I'll see you back home. It's been a rough enough day without your mouth music. Sounds like you're gargling with acid.'

I could have taken the hump with Dad, but hey: Out early from work and paid too! *Hakuna Metata,* I hummed. Into myself this time. Didn't want old Pops changing his mind. Not before I hopped the chalked ghost of the man whose misfortune had improved my Saturday no end.

Wonder if he's dead, concern suddenly hit me. Flickered. Momentarily. Infinitesimally. Till I recalled what Marjory had said about the hammer victim: *Big-time crack dealer. Scum.*

I shivered then, like something nasty I couldn't see had brushed up against me.

Brrr. Definitely time for some choccy therapy, I decided.

But be good. Only a Mars Bar and a celeb mag. Not piles of chocolate I cautioned myself.

At the newsagent's counter I'd a Mars Bar and a Snickers in one hand, and was swithering over Maltesers or Minstrels or both, and I'd have bought them all if an arm hadn't reached across me.

'Some days you gotta have a sugar fix, yeah?' this voice – male – whispered to me. A soft, tan sleeve just and no more brushed against the front of my jacket. I caught a waft of suede mixed with fabulous aftershave. It was a heady combination.

Brrr.

For the second time in five minutes I shivered. Deliciously. Had to lunge for the sweet counter to stay upright. As I moved forward, my outstretched hand accidentally shunted the fingers on the end of the soft suede sleeve. This was just as they were closing on the packet of Minstrels I fancied.

Was I mortified! Two blast furnaces fired up in my cheeks like they always do when I'm embarrassed, their instant heat throbbing my face scarlet. And this was *before* the person attached to the fingers and the soft suede sleeve held the Minstrels out to me.

'Sorry. Last packet. You're before me. These your favourites too? Hey, we could share?'

I was surprised the skin wasn't melting off this sweet-talking guy's face. Because now I was radiating enough thermal energy to liquidise every bar of chocolate on the counter. And sweet-talking guy was so close. Close enough for me to notice he was about two inches taller than I am, which made him six feet plus, and that his pale grey eyes were flecked with streaks of blue, and his lashes were black and longer and thicker than mine, and his cheekbones were high, and his skin was clear and slightly tanned, and his smile was so broad, and his teeth so straight and white and perfect that I wished I'd checked the overlaps and crannies in my own for Brazil nut debris. Oh, and popped a stick of super-mint chuggy before I left Dad's shop.

Because this guy . . .

This *guy* pushing back his dense, goldy-fair hair while he grinned at me was so *cute* . . .

Honestly. Why **are** *you grinning at me, exactly? Talking about sharing Minstrels,* I was thinking while he chuckled, 'I try not to bite through the hard shell, but it's too tempting.'

And I was trying to place the ever-so-faint accent that made him pronounce his t's and roll his r's in a way that looped frizzles up and down the back of my neck, and made me want to beg him to keep on talking to me even though a voice in my head was niggling: *This is bonkers, Clod. Handsome dudes never sidle up beside big ginga gals out of the blue and confess,* 'I can't resist the chocolate in the middle of a Minstrel.'

Come on sweet-talking guy. Look at me properly. Then rewind. Do us both a favour. Especially me. Make the world go back to normal. Coz this ain't right.

That's what the *Get-a-grip, Clod!* voice of reason inside my brain kept insisting. Even when this utter *hottie* cupped his hand round my elbow and steered me out of the queue we were holding up to continue our conversation. Even when he introduced himself.

'I'm Stefan.'

That was when we shook hands. And he took my right paw in both of his. Clasped it tight even though it was clammy with sweat and a bit sticky from the chocolate Brazils. But he didn't let go. Squeezed.

'And you are?'

'Claudia,' I told him. 'But I'm called Clod. Y'know, Clod by name, Clod by na–'

'Claudia. Like Schiffer. Supermodel,' Stefan interrupted me by leaning forward and kissing the salty base of my palm.

(Note to self: Finally. 17¾ years old. First kiss. And about time too.) His lips barely made contact with my skin, but Stefan had damaged me for life. My poor heart felt like it wanted to gallop free of my ribcage. I couldn't regulate my breathing. My kneecaps were visibly vibrating through my trousers and all the blood in my upper body seemed to be relocating to my groin. That's why I didn't hear a word that I nodded and smiled at in the – well, it could have been twenty seconds or twenty years Stefan chatted to me following his killer kiss before I was aware of hearing normally. In fact I didn't even think I *was* hearing

normally yet. This

donk, donk, donk

bass-line seemed to be throbbing in the space between us

donk donk donk

Thinking that my body was undergoing some kind of cardiac trauma due to the shock of being kissed by a male who wasn't a blood relative, I shook my head to make the throb go away. But it only happened again. Louder:

donk donk donk

Louder still when Stefan pulled a mobile from the inside pocket of his jacket. Cut the call just as I was able to Name That Ringtone: *Another One Bites The Dust.* A classic blast of bass and Freddy gristle.

'Haven't I spied you working in the optician's?' Stefan gave me his bling smile as he slipped the phone back in his pocket without – I noticed – bothering to check the caller.

'Me? You've seen *me*?' I couldn't believe what I was hearing. *A guy like you?* I was ready to add but Stefan was talking over me.

'What the hell happened there today?' he asked,

joining the sweet queue again. 'I heard a woman saying someone died. Did you see it?'

clod's first date

We shared the packet of Minstrels outside the news-agent's. Not exactly 50-50, if I'm being honest. I always eat two at once, gannet that I am. But I don't think Stefan noticed.

Nah. He seemed obsessed by the fact that I'd been all alone-o inside Quinn's when the hammer drama kicked off. But not obsessed in a nosey old Mulleny kind of way. No. And definitely *not* because he was gagging for gory details involving blood or smashed teeth or broken bones. Stefan only wanted to know about the hammer attack because – *sweetie pie* – he was worried about the effect it might have had on little old *moi.*

'You must have been *terrified,* Claudia. You poor thing,' Stefan put his hands on my shoulders and looked deep into my eyes. When he sighed his breath smelt of chocolate. Mmmm.

'Two men smash up another while you're stuck in

the optician's all by yourself? Just you? No customers?'

As he probed me with questions, Stefan stroked my shoulders.

'Yeah, only me. Dad was on lunch,' I shrugged, mainly to nestle against the weight of his hands. *This is unreal,* I was still thinking. From where I stood, practically in Stefan's lovin' arms, eating chocolate to boot (Does life get any sweeter?) I could see our shop. It was garlanded with police tape. Dad was outside it, shaking his head.

'Look, Pa. Ain't such a crap day after all. I'm being chatted up! And not by a gargoyle!' I was tempted to yell out. But I don't think Dad would have given me thumbs-up right now. He'd his back to me and his thumbs were otherwise engaged. One was jabbing at the mess on his window, the other at some noddy-suit huddled over the outline of the hammered man plucking the ground with tweezers.

'Just as well Dad was elsewhere,' I told Stefan, pointing him to the scene. 'He'd've tried to stop the attack. Got himself whacked by a pair of hammer-psychos, knowing him.'

'You saw them?'

'Huh?'

Stefan's fingers stopped stroking. Pressed into my collarbone instead. 'You saw the guys who did this? Have you given a statement to the police?' Stefan's grip grew less gentle as he spoke. I twisted to free myself.

'Hey –'

'Oh, Claudia. Sorry. It's just that –' Stefan's fingers relaxed. He ran his hands the length of my arms till he reached my sticky paws. His knees crooked so his pale grey eyes were level with mine. The little smirk he shrugged me dimpled at the left side of his mouth. Made him look baby-faced.

'Sometimes,' he said, while I tried to guess his age – *Eighteen? Twenty? More? Impossible to tell* – 'you hear about people helping the police and they end up . . .'

'End up what?'

donk donk donk

When the phone in Stefan's soft suede jacket pulsed, I felt the vibration in our joined hands. Like we shared a heartbeat:

donk donk donk,
Another One Bites The . . .
donk donk donk . . .

'Don't you ever answer that?' I nodded at the sound. 'Hate to be *your* girlfriend.'

'How can you stay that, Claudia? D'you want to break my heart, babes?' Stefan let go my hands to dig out his phone. He cut the call again. Then he thumbed his menu button. Handed the mobile to me. It was a tiny, sexy slip of stainless steel. State of the art.

CLAUDIA – ADD NUMBER: its screen winked.

So I accepted the invitation. Good thing too.

My own mobile rang as soon as I handed his back.

'Hi? Claudia? It's Stefan. Can I see you later? Please say yes, babes?' Before I'd even fished mine out my pocket Stefan's eyes were pleading over his tiny, sexy mobile, while my tinny non-polyphonic ringtone embarrassed me by playing *I Am the Walrus*.

nothing to wear

'You don't know *anything* about this guy, you nutter,' I giggled, floating home after agreeing to meet Stefan outside the Underground. Couple of hours from now.

'You don't know what age he is, where he lives, what he does, his surname . . . So what, he's *GORGEOUS*. Live dangerously,' I announced at volume to a small boy zigzagging towards me on a scooter, head down. He wouldn't be doing that again. Not without a helmet. Not to *my* pelvis anyway.

Yeah, live dangerously, I decided. What else was I going to do? Get Starsky and Hutch to run a police check on Stefan?

Hire manly Marjory as my bodyguard?

Was I going to send Stefan a text questionnaire:

Excuse me, most gorgeous guy
I've ever met. See before you

go down in history as my FIRST
and ONLY date, d'you mind
ticking the following boxes to
disclose whether or not you
are:

A. A psycho axe-murderer.

B. The Devil in a suede jacket.

C. Just after me for my body.
(Ooooh yes please!)

It wasn't as if five foot ten, size-nine-footed Desperate Dinas like Clodhopper Quinn here could be choosers. And frankly, with a back-story like mine in romance, two hours with a psycho axe-murderer was a score in my book! I'd make sure me and Stefan stuck to public, well-lit areas. I'd even ask him to leave his axe behind the bar. Politely, of course.

'Anyway, we're only going for a *drink,*' I reassured the showered, naked hefty slad of flesh filling my bedroom table mirror. Then I groaned. Aye and it would be ONE drink, too. Then *Time, gentlemen, please;* the state of me.

'Nice knowing you Claudia,' as I imagined Stefan's eyes scrutinising what I was seeing right now, I also heard his voice in my head. It was giving me the brush-off in the slightest foreign accent – Swedish? Danish maybe? Sexy whatever it was. 'Specially when it was calling me 'babes'.

'Sorry, Claudia. I think you've a brilliant personality but you and I just aren't right for each . . .'

In a Scandinaviany whisper, I armoured my reflection for the inevitable: *'Clod, you're fired!'*

Yeah. I'd give my relationship with Stefan half an hour tops. Before he acted on impulse again with a lassie, he'd be booking in at my dad's for an ocular oil-change and service.

Oh well, being somebody's babes was fun while it lasted. I consoled myself with the half-eaten Jaffa-cake I found next to my bed. Hardly the comfort food I needed. Especially when I opened my wardrobe and discovered that the Special Outfit Fairy I'd made a wish for in the shower wasn't flitting about inside waving her magic wand over the latest *Who's Looking at Me, Anyway? Collection*.

For my FIRST and ONLY Date I'd a choice of changing into my ONE and ONLY pair of jeans that zipped up properly. Either that, or I squeezed back into the Quinn's Family Eyecare navy polyester uniform trousers I'd been wearing all day. These are hideous on me. So hideous that *even* Mum, a diplomat with thirty years' experience of telling people what they really look like in specs that do nothing for them, and someone who never, ever, *ever* comments on my statuesque dimensions suggested, when Dad insisted I wore them for work, 'Sean, they're not exactly the best cut when you're as well-built as our Cloddy.'

My last-resort sartorial options were the Ozzy Osbourne-style joggies I favoured for slobbing round the house in . . . or – Wait for it – my school skirt. It was pleated. Shiny-seated. Brown. And in the dirty laundry basket.

'So I have *nothing* decent to wear.'

For the First Time in my entire life I wished my mum was here to deal with my First Ever Fashion Crisis. Not in Melbourne. Waiting for my brother's wife to finally make her a glammy granny and me an auntie. Mum would have celebrated my Nothing To Wear Emergency by taking me on the kind of Ultimate Shopping Spree she's prayed and dreamed her Clyde-Built Disappointment Of A Daughter might desire some day.

But Mum wasn't here. Nor any handy fashionista girlfriends with plus-size clothes to lend. Not *any* mates, come to think of it, with my best mate Georgina on the other side of the globe just when I needed her most. Alas and alack. But I'd no time to dwell on my lone-o status. Not right now when I'd an hour max to get myself tarted up. Either that or I dingied Stefan. With a no-show, or a text:

Srry.Cnt mke 2nite.Bi.

That's why, as a last resort, I ended up in Mum's room, plundering her wardrobe.

How sad was that? My mum's forty-nine, for God's sake. Size twelve body. Size four feet. She's what you'd call 'laydee-like', as in USA First-Lady-like. Into knee-length dresses and killer heels, or twinky little skirt-suits like Jackie O used to wear. She hates women in trousers. Believes there should a law making it a fashion crime, punishable by public flogging in Top Shop, for anyone over sixteen to be caught wearing jeans. Over age and *size* sixteen. Which means Mum's Law would criminalise me. Her Big Clod Of An Only Daughter.

Look at you. Complete and utter lost cause, I could hear Mum right now. Chanting her mantra of disappointment at the sight of me squeezed into her Ralph Lauren Little Black Dress. I was wearing it skin-tight (not by choice) and tunic-style over my tatty jeans.

'But I'm in a frock, Mum. Look!' I picked Mum's wedding photo from her bedside table. Panned it over me on the off-chance it was a portal to Down Under. 'And I'm going on a date. This guy. He just started talking to me . . .'

Picked me up in the newsagent's . . .

Mum's twenty-year-old eyes stared thirty years into the future. Locked on mine.

Hold on, Cloddy, the eyes in the photo seemed to narrow slightly.

Where *did you meet this, this . . .?*

Stefan, he's called. He just picked me up . . .

All sounds a bit sudden, Cloddy. Nice boys just don't . . . You just make sure you . . . And let me see what you're wearing? Why are you all unbuttoned like that?

I clamped my hand to the opening of Mum's dress, hiding the spill of my boobs. When I'd put it on, I left the front deliberately undone.

And why wouldn't I flash my two best assets?

Rather than make myself as decent as the innocent bride-smile on my mum's face, I placed the wedding photo face-down on her bed.

Well you just better watch yourself, Cloddy. I imagined I could still hear Mum's duvet-muffled warning. *D'you know where this Stefan's taking you? Find out and tell your dad, OK? Is there money on your phone? D'you have enough for a taxi? You won't be leaving drinks with this fella if you go to the Ladies –*

Leave my drink? I wouldn't be out long enough to need a pee, I convinced myself, swiping one of Mum's scarlet lipsticks randomly over my mouth. Then swiping my mouth clean again. Who was I kidding?

Trying to scrub up. There'd be no need to tell Dad *nothing* about my plans! This date would be history before Dad's standing Saturday evening rendezvous with *Doctor Who* was over. He wouldn't even known I was out and I'd be back in my room. Joggies on.

So don't worry, Mum. I was locking the front door, walking up the garden path, talking aloud to myself. I confess I tend to do that when I'm alone on the lane that connects our house to the street. Either talk or hum. Helps take my mind off how far us Quinns live from the nearest neighbour . . .

Anyway – phew – I could see the street now. That's where I caught a final glimpse of myself in the privacy windows and spotless paintwork of another of those massive yummy-mummy cars. Must have had dodgy Sat Nav or something to be parked, engine running, at the end of our lane.

Before I could decide if it was the same make of car as the one Dad and the Mullens walked out in front of earlier, it sleeked away. My reflection tracked along its nearside. It was not an inspiring sight. *Seventeen, and your First and Only date'll be a speed date,* I bet myself a fish supper on the way home. In that time I'd be lucky to get Stefan's surname, let alone his life history.

the glasgow speakeasy

But I lost my bet.

No fish supper.

Still, even *I* wouldn't have managed it. Not after Caesar salad, fillet steak with mash, and a medley of fine Italian ice creams. All washed down with champagne. Two bottles Stefan and I necked between us. Well, I necked. Mainly.

Good going for a debut date. Not that I could personally compare the situation with anything.

All I knew was the first night my best pal Georgina stepped out with Amazingly Intelligent Adrian (who has since turned out to be The Love Of Her Life) they shared a smoothie in Starbucks. Cost and straw. By the way, on the subject of Georgina, walking to the Underground to meet Stefan I reminded myself not to forget every juicy detail of my date, so I could debrief Georgina later. Not face to face, alas and alack, but in the weekly email I'd be sending through cyberspace to a godforsaken village in India or Africa or somewhere flyblown with no running water and sporadic electricity. That's where Georgina, my Bestest Buddy, was off gap-yearing. With Amazingly Intelligent Adrian instead of Amazingly Unintelligent *moi*. Double alas and alack! Mum's right: I really was Clod by name and Clod by nature. After all, the single solitary significant thing I'd managed to do properly and thoroughly in my life thus far was fail. All my big exams last year. Spectacularly 100 per cent result! Ds and No Mentions. Which is why I was stuck in sixth form doing five resits without a decent mate for company. Hating every minute of it. But that's another story . . .

Far more interesting was what I'd be reporting to Georgina in this week's bulletin from the Civilised City:

How Stefan – black jacket, black t-shirt, still full-on gorgeous – was already waiting for me outside the Underground. A rose poking out the back pocket of his jeans. OK: cheesy gesture, but Stefan just about got away with it. The rose was for me, after all.

As Stefan passed the flower over he kissed me on both cheeks – *mwa, mwa, mwa* – Continental-style, and tickled my nose with its petals so my knees buckled. Then he took my hand and said, 'You look *un*believable, babes.'

With attention like that from a dreamboat who did not appear to be paying some kind of forfeit, no wonder the night turned into something of a blur. Even before I partook of intoxicating refreshment I realised I wouldn't even be able to give Georgina the name of the restaurant we went to. Or where it was. Although my problems with the alcohol-free portion of the evening happened because for most of the taxi-ride to an address I didn't catch Stefan giving the driver, I'd my eyes on the meter and my mind doing mental subtraction on the twenty-quid note I'd shoved in my back pocket. I've a notion I was humming again too. Just a touch of *Tragedy*. That's until the fare ticked up to £18.60 and I must have stopped breathing or something. Stefan chuckled and covered my eyes with his hand.

'Hey. Relax. Blink. Exhale. Never worry about a

thing when I'm taking care of you, babes,' he murmured, sliding his hand from my eyes to my cheek. Holding it there so I nearly swooned from the heat and scent of his skin and the hint of cologne on his wrist. A perfect moment if I hadn't had to share it with the ugly little snake tattooed there, it's forked tongue flicking out as flame instead of flesh.

Still, despite the disappointment of my sweet-talking guy having one imperfection (I HATE tattoos), as far as I was concerned I was in heaven already when our taxi chugged up a cobbled lane and dropped us outside an archway sprinkled in fairy lights. Lazy jazz guitar drifted up to greet me and Stefan as, fingers threaded through mine, he led me down down down a steep, uneven stairway.

'Where are we?' I asked when we were standing in pitch darkness waiting for someone to answer three hard raps Stefan had given a door I could only presume was there.

'Here,' he said as the door opened and the jazzy music grew louder. I'd stepped into a smallish room. It was low ceilinged. Candlelit. Partitioned into four or five booths, each one draped with thick, spangled voile through which I could barely distinguish shapes: dark jackets and bulky outlines of men. The glint of a bracelet or necklace against bare, female skin. Not to mention the shock glow of an illegal indoors cigarette. From each booth voices rose and fell in chatter. Adult voices: pealing females, muttering men. No one my age. Or Stefan's, for that matter. *Though I can't figure his age. And this is a grown-up place,* I decided, aware of crystal and cutlery and laughter tinkling and chinking to accompany two musicians in sharp suits and pork pie hats. In the furthest corner of the room one brushed a drumkit, his eyes permanently closed. The other – a dead ringer for BB King – riffed on a massive chrome guitar.

'Where are we? A Glasgow speakeasy?' I asked, obeying the beckon of a spherical tuxedoed man who was at least a foot smaller than myself. Without a word he marched me and Stefan into the only unoccupied booth.

'Why d'you ask? Don't you like? You more a Burger King girl?' Even as he made the suggestion, and before I could snap back – a tad offended – *Do I look like a Burger King girl?* Stefan was tugging me down to sit beside him. So I plomped on to a plush bench of padded velvet. On the table in front of me a bottle of champagne peeked from an ice bucket. It was already open.

'No . . . it's just it's all . . . amazing.' I took the glass Mr Tuxedo filled and Stefan handed to me. *It's a sophisticated, 100-per-cent-non-Clod Quinn kind of a place,* I was thinking, *and here's me in my jeans and no make-up . . .*

'Well then, if you're happy, does it matter where we are?' Stefan was smiling broadly at Mr Tuxedo. By the time I'd looked up to see if he was included in our conversation, we were alone in the booth.

'To us,' Stefan raised his glass. 'Cheers! Saluti! Mazel Tof!' he grinned, necking his champagne in a oner. Not knowing any better, Coke being the only fizzy drink I normally swig with my din-dins, I did the same. Course it went straight to my head.

'Zat one of your customs? Sloshing back the bev?'

Before I'd even put down my empty glass I was

giggling, trying not to snot champagne bubbles.

'Customs?' Stefan was frowning. Refilling my glass. Guiding it to my lips.

'Y'know: Mazel Tof! Down the hatch! One of your foreign customs,' I sloshed another toast at Stefan, 'Coz you're not from . . . y'know? Here.' When I waved my drink in the air, I managed to sluice wine all down my hand and over the sleeve of Mum's Ralph Lauren dress. 'You're Norwegian or Dutch or Swedey or . . .?'

'My passport says British Citizen, clumsy Claudia.' Stefan interrupted my list of fantasy Nordic types – before I could suggest 'Finnish' or 'Icelandic' or 'Viking' – by taking my wet hand in his and kissing it. That was enough to make me forget what I was asking him about. But when he started to lick drips of champagne from the inside of my wrist . . .

dishing the family dirt

Well, frankly, a move like that on a girl who's never been licked by a stray dog with halitosis let alone a buff sweetie like Stefan was enough to scramble my head completely.

What did I care who this guy was.

We were here.

This date was probably all going to turn out to be a horrible mistake on his part. Or else I was having one of my occasional magic dreams that make up for the Crapness Of Being Clod. Whatever. All that mattered was I really liked Stefan and he seemed – even temporarily – into me. Enough, at least, to stroke my hair with his thumbnail then run it from my neck to my collarbone. Zigzag it down to where I hadn't buttoned Mum's dress . . .

Phew! Just as well the food arrived.

Funny, that's what Stefan said, adding, 'Phew.

You're something else, Claudia. And I want to find out all about you tonight.'

Then the tuxedoed sphere put down our starters.

'Thank you, Radec,' Stefan told him.

I couldn't recall having seen a menu at this point, let alone ordering any chow from – Radox? Radish? Radec? What kind of name was that anyway?

But maybe I *had* ordered without realising. Things were moving so quickly here. Too quickly. I wanted Stefan to dish me some facts about himself, but somehow the evening passed with me doing all the blethering. Not deliberately though: I'm anything but a gasbag. Ask any teacher who's put up with my surly silences over the years. A cocktail of nerves and alcohol must have loosened my tongue. Combined with the fact that Stefan played the perfect gentleman.

'No, no, no,' he kept insisting whenever I asked him stuff like, 'So where d'you live? Who's in your family?'

'Ladies first, Claudia,' he'd chuckle. 'Go on.'

With prompting like that, not to mention Stefan feeding me bites of rare steak from his plate and spooning ice cream into my cakehole, it was understandable I ended up spilling most of the Quinn family beans in the course of three courses. Stefan learned not only that my big-shot big brother businessman Neil in Melbourne had a low sperm count, but that his wife Margaret-Mary had a hairy face (yes, Bless Me Father, I did reveal my pet name for her), and my dad had been recently diagnosed with high blood pressure and thought Coldplay were class. By the time our dessert plates had been cleared away and I was slurping either my fourth or fifth glass of champers, Stefan was up to date on my garbageness at school and Mum's decision to stay Down Under for at least a week after Neil's baby came.

'Sh' might not be home f'r'ages yet,' I told Stefan through truffles so rich and buttery that even an expert like myself wouldn't hazard a guess at their fat content. 'Dad's still here coz Mum thinks I can't be trusted to shut the fridge, let alone a front door. "You know I love you to bits but you're hardly the brightest light on the Christmas tree, Cloddy –"'

'Oh, that's unfair,' Stefan put his finger to my lips before I could go on running myself down in Mum's disappointed voice. 'You're left in charge of a *business* on your own. You handle money. Need to be smart for that. You deal with customers. Complaints –'

'Yeah, but one of the other receptionists is usually there. I just sit about. Answer the phone. File. Dad's short-staffed just now. Normally I only cover lunchtime alone. Quietest time. Safe enough –'

'Hey not today. Bloody hell, Claudia.' Stefan, face very close to mine, shook his head like he wanted to disperse something unpleasant inside it. 'I know you haven't talked about . . . y'know . . . earlier . . .?' Stefan's hand covered my own, 'but, I've been going over and over it. You must have been *terrified*. Maybe you want to tell me more? I'm a great listener –'

The lull in our chat was the first of our date, Stefan holding open a space for me to relive something – well, to tell the truth, something I'd pushed to the back of my mind for the last few hours.

What's to talk about? I was thinking, *I'm far more interested in the way your hair falls over your eyes when you look down, Stefan. Let's talk about that. And maybe about me running my fingers through it while you snog me dizzy . . .*

In the silence between us, Stefan let go my hand. Opened his wallet, sifting though a healthy selection of plastic friends. Holy Moley, the guy had accounts with every bank in the UK! When he slid out one of those special Red AMEX cards Saint Bono invented for Minted People, I couldn't stop myself blurting, 'Y'a millionaire or something?'

'Just like good causes,' Stefan's shrug was bashful enough to stop me coming right out and asking him exactly what he did to be flush enough for a Red AMEX. Any AMEX. A guy his age – whatever that was.

D'you rob banks or old ladies? Deal crack? I might have said.

But Radec was by my side like he could smell a tip.

'All yours, my friend,' Stefan slipped the card into Radec's breast pocket. When he patted it with the flat of his hand the gesture was a dismissal as well as payment. His eyes, never leaving mine, were serious. Made him seem older all of a sudden.

'Claudia,' he whispered although we were quite alone, 'I've got to ask: You know when that man was hammered, d'you really not see the pair who did it?

Their faces? Because you know the cops, and the SOCOs – y'know the Scene Of Crime Officers? – they were making a fingertip search. Dusting for prints. That's major forensics. They must want those guys badly. So if you got an ID on them –'

'But I didn't.' My interruption sounded like panic. *Change the subject,* I was thinking. This conversation was giving me indigestion.

'How come you're up on all the jargon: SOCOs, fingertip searches? You a gangster or something?' I chuckled into my champagne, peeking at Stefan over the top of my glass.

'Just big into violent crime,' he answered, waiting till my own eyes widened before chuckling, 'fiction, I mean. Lee Child. Ian Rankin. Michael Collins. Hey. Got you going there, Claudia. How could a babyface like me be a bad guy?'

Stefan's arm went round my shoulders and he pulled me close against his T-shirt, holding me to the muscles in his chest. Nothing baby-faced about them! Since this was the first time I'd been hugged by any male other than Dad or my uncle Mike or in dreams,

I'd happily have stayed in that position until undertakers prised my bones free. But my bliss was fleeting. Stefan noogied my head like I was his kid brother. Released me, then returned to the one topic of conversation I'd rather end.

'Seriously,' he said seriously, 'what'll you tell the cops if they come back to question you –?'

'But the cops won't,' I shrugged. 'Less the guy dies. Jeez. That'd be a murder I'd s–' I'd my hand over my mouth. With the way my head was spinning I wasn't sure if I was clamping it shut to stop what I was about to admit to Stefan, or a shock reflex at the realisation that I'd *actually* witnessed a man thumped to death. Or maybe I just didn't want Stefan to hear me burp.

'Babes,' Stefan took my hand. 'If that guy dies you'll be grilled bigtime. And the papers might get your name. Your picture. Would you tell the cops more? Can you? Because people don't always realise how much they've seen. New detail might come in flashback. Subconscious mind and all that. Incredible stuff goes on in there.'

Stefan tapped the middle of my forehead as he

tipped the dregs of the second bottle of champagne into my empty glass. My just-about-conscious mind was trying to unscramble the thought:

You clever I bet psychology are student Aha!

and turn it into a sequence of words, but everything in my head had slurred and anyway, Stefan's phone –

'Donked,' I was going to say.

But he must have changed the ringtone or something. This time it played the whistley assassin tune from *Kill Bill.*

And actually the phone he pulled out wasn't the stainless steel one he'd used earlier. At least I didn't think it was. Half-cut in a dim booth I could barely focus on anything when Stefan pecked me on the top of the head. 'Sorry, babes. Gotta take this. Little bit of business. I'll slip upstairs for a better signal. Don't go away.'

As if, I thought, realising I could do with nipping to the loo. Stumbling about a candlelit room was easier said than done with a bottle and a half of champagne sloshing inside me. After lurching through a voile curtain which concealed an old man snogging the face off some woman half his age – *Excuse me!* – Radec gestured me unsmilingly to the door I wanted. 'Lookayu, Claudia Quinn,' I slumped on the toilet seat and scolded the flushed, twin girls with plunging blotchy necklines I could see in the mirror. 'Cupletely pissed. Yak yak yak, ya big bore.'

When I flung my arms towards the twin me's in disgust I must have lost my balance. Hit the floor. Couldn't seem to lift myself off it. I was safer staying put anyway. Bones felt like they'd turned to concrete. Couldn't move them. And the world was twirling faster and faster . . .

The next thing I remembered was a sensation of being hoisted upright by several arms. None of them gentle. Nor were any of the male voices who sniggered comments in a language I'd never heard before. And neighed to each other. And *definitely* not gentle was the hand that thwacked my backside as I was slung over someone's shoulder. Slowly and haltingly shifted up a flight of stairs.

The vehicle I was poured into at the top can't have been a regular taxi. It was too sleek and well-upholstered, and anyway Glasgow taxis refuse paralytic fares in case they puke. They don't blast out foreign speed-folk violin music to their passengers either, which the driver sings along to at the top of his voice. So who knows what brought me home.

Or who.

My eyes wouldn't open, you see. Lids were paralysed. Lead dead-weights, same as my lips and my tongue and my voice.

So all I know is that my companion on the ride home was some bloke whose shouted conversation with the driver wasn't in English or school French.

Whoever he was, he somehow knew my address, even though I'm sure it was about the only personal detail I hadn't given Stefan.

And he went through my jeans for my keys.

And he must have been stealthy as a cat-burglar. Not to mention chivalry itself.

Because when I woke with the hangover from Hell's Hell – (*Note to self: Nothing glam about Champagne –*

it's poison). I was in my bed and under the covers. Shoes off, but fully dressed. My hands were crossed, Sleeping Beauty-style, over my chest, and the rose Stefan had given me was clasped in them. On my bedside table someone had left me a mug of water, two paracetamol and a strategically placed basin.

All this had happened without my dad hearing a sound.

9

to hell and beyond

I knew Dad must have been oblivious to his only daughter being carried home bladdered and put to bed by at least one strange man, because there was a note outside my bedroom door. I slipped on it when I finally groped from my room thinking a shower might drown the evil invisible goblin drumming my temples with a pickaxe. It didn't. And I won't go into details about how sick I was. Suffice to say my three-course meal tasted better on the way down than it did on the way up.

Too hungover to even dry myself, I crawled back into bed with Dad's note. Had to crawl back out again to find sunglasses. The white paper left my eyes feeling like they were being skewered by red-hot knitting needles.

Morning my precious Clod,

Dad had written.

6 a.m. on my day off.
Your snoring woke me, sweetness. Thank you.
And I thought your
humming was bad!!!
I'm away fishing for some peace and quiet.
Perthshire. Meeting your
Uncle Mike half way.
See you tonight.
Pa.
PS — Had a Senior Moment and mislaid my
VISA card. Sure it was in my wallet. Any
chance you'll have a snuffle around?

'Later,' I groaned, curling into a ball of misery. My intention was to die, and I probably did for a few hours or weeks or years – who knows – until a bell started ringing and ringing and ringing in my head: **dingdongdongdongdingdong.**

The sound was far away at first, so I ignored it, but it didn't quit: instead it became louder, taking the throb in my temples to new realms of pain: **dingdingdingdongdingdong.**

Then it grew even more annoying. It was being accompanied by non-stop banging.

'I will never drink champagne again in my life,' were the first words I croaked when I realised I was not actually in a queue outside the Pearly Gates. No, I was in Hell where someone had already tortured me by supergluei ng my tongue to my bottom teeth, Artexing the roof of my mouth and sandpapering my throat.

It was dark in Hell, too, and I was beginning to hear voices in my head on top of infernal ringing and banging.

'Hello, Claudia Quinn. Anyone home?' the voices – male and female, one as deep as the other – were calling.

I whimpered and rolled over. Ouch! Something sharp pierced my bare bahooky. That shot me out of bed. I'd been sobered up by the thorns on Stefan's red rose.

So I wasn't in Hell after all. And actually, once I was on my feet, the evil invisible goblin seemed to have tired of pounding my head quite so hard. Even better, the horrible ringing had stopped, although the banging continued. And the voices were still shouting.

'Hey? Anyone home? Police here.'

'No sign of life, sir, we'll try later.' I recognised Marjory's voice. Then everything grew quiet.

'P'lice?'

Up in my room I froze in front of my mirror, a naked lifesize statue: Hungover Lassie with Glass of Water. 21st Century. Alabaster. Artist unknown.

There were heavy footsteps crunching a retreat down our long gravel path. The click and squeak of our annoying gate at the far end. A car started before three doors slammed and wheels pulled away on wet tarmac. Now there was silence.

Except for my whisper in the dark.

'The hammer guy. He's dead.'

I was covered in goosepimples, my heart racing.

'What happens now?' I gulped just as *I Am the Walrus* rattled tinnily from the chair on which the jacket I'd worn last night had been draped.

10

better safe than sorry

'Smart place, babes. A bit lonely, though.'

Less than five minutes after phoning to give me a five-minute warning – 'I need to see you, Claudia' – and in way less than I needed to spruce up, Stefan stood in the centre of our living room.

He's back to see me. This is unbelievable.

It wasn't a cruel mirage either. Even after I pinched myself, Stefan was still there. The pointy cowboy boots he was wearing sank into the fancy rug Mum didn't allow footwear on, leaving their outline on the pile. The Man in Black he was today – *Hello, I'm Johnny Cash* – his full-length, rain-spotted leather coat scenting the room deliciously when it swung behind the rest of him to examine Mum's display-cabinet crammed with antique perfume bottles, then the horrible cow-specked Highland landscapes Dad reckoned would fund his retirement.

'Hope Mr and Mrs Claudia are well insured. There's

fair brass 'ere, lass.' Stefan didn't quite pull off the Ee-By-Gum accent he was attempting. It jarred with his own. Never mind. I forgave him because when he flung himself down on our sofa he grabbed the belt of my dressing gown. Pulled me next to him.

'Show me again,' he said. His hand went from my knee to the business card I'd scooped from the front door when I opened it to let Stefan in.

Starsky-Stark's name and mobile number were on one side. The back read:

> Ms Quinn,
> Called 4.30pm.
> Will try again after 7.30pm unless you arrange alternative time.
> Need to talk to you.

'Think that means this is a mudder enquiry?' I said 'mudder enquiry' like they always do on *Taggart* while Stefan read the card.

'I better phone. See what the cops want –' I went on. But Stefan interrupted.

'You mean phone *now*? When I'm here to see you? Take you out for tea? Don't think so –' Stefan was grinning at me when he plucked the DCI's calling card from my hand. He held it at arm's length by the tiniest corner like it was something contaminated. When he dropped it to the carpet his smile dropped too. He shook his head slowly. Scowled.

'Never tell cops *anything*, babes,' Stefan said in a low voice. 'They're bad news, every last one of them. Bad guys with badges my father calls them –'

Stefan had hunched forward on the sofa. While he spoke he ground the DCI's card under the sole of his pointy boot. Because his hair had flopped all thick and blondly over his face it felt like he'd curtained himself away from me.

Must have some private grief with the cops, I decided, also trying to figure if Stefan's hair was naturally streaked with so many shades of blonde, or subtly highlighted.

Expensively subtly highlighted if it was.

But I didn't feel it was my place to ask for details about either. Too personal. Nah. Didn't know Stefan well enough yet, did I? Nor did I feel this was quite the time to reveal that my totally favourite uncle, Dad's younger bro and fishing partner, Mike, was also a cop – a big-shot one too – Chief Super somewhere up . . .

Where the heck was it again? Smelly port . . . North East . . . where all the canneries and prawns . . . Near Peterhead maybe? Could never remember.

More heroin than herring coming in these days. And Eastern European labour . . . Those were the only facts that came back to me right now about Uncle Super Mike's patch. Especially when my head was still as mushy as wet wool and The Most Gorgeous Guy I'd Ever Met had his thigh pressed the length of mine. Only when I gave up nipping my brain for the name of Uncle Mike's station did I realise Stefan was tapping the back of my hand with his fingertips.

'. . . Anyway you need a change of scene right now. You're looking a bit fragile. No wonder. Still paying for dancing on those tables and ordering those cocktails after your champagne, aren't you? I did warn you –'

'I was dancing?' *I never dance.*

'Singing too. All the way home in the taxi. Up your

path. Shaking your keys. Can't believe you didn't wake your dad up.'

'I was singing?' *And I wasn't carried out the restaurant? You saw me home? How come I don't remember?*

'Babes, you are a wild one. Mind you,' Stefan smacked my thigh till I stopped wading through my hangover for the source of it, 'you look like you could do with some fresh air. Won't get any of that talking to the law. So go get dressed for me. Let't get out of here before the day's gone.

'Babes.'

Stefan was calling me that more and more. *And here's me like death's ugly sister warmed up.*

That's what I was thinking while I pulled out every item of clothing I possessed. All my tops were black. Baggy. Sloganed with back-off snarls:

Have a Nice Day, Asshole.

BIG GIRLS DON'T CARE.

'Bloody nothing decent,' I realised, plunging through the pile of washed-out black cotton on my bed.

'See you in five. Taking you somewhere nice,'

Stefan had told me downstairs. I'd left him there on the sofa watching Andy Murray giving John McEnroe the grumpy monotone treatment on *Sky Sport*. Somewhere nice?

With a wardrobe full of gear that never went anywhere nice, I panicked. Dashed through to Mum and Dad's room in my undies: big grey-white bra, bigger greyer-white pants. Built for support and containment, they were about as removed from the scanties barely covering those models who've made M&S underwear sexy again as I am from Elizabeth Jagger. So God knows what Stefan thought when he spun round from Mum's dressing table.

(Note to self: Keep a decent set of frillies for Emergency Use Only. Wash separately.)

I was so mortified at Stefan copping an eyeful of all my blubby bits it only *just* crossed my mind that he was somewhere he Definitely Shouldn't Be.

Naughty boy.

Trespassing in my mumsie's bedroom.

I just yelped. Grabbed the first white shirt hanging in Dad's wardrobe.

Fled to my own room.

'Hey, Claudia.' Stefan's fingertips were brushing my door. 'Sorry. Sorry. That wasn't what it looked like. I was looking for your little boy's room. I'm just a vain bugger. Saw that big long mirror and nipped in to check myself out –'

Stefan was half-laughing his apology. Still brushing at the door. 'Clau-dia!' When I didn't answer, his voice sing-songed like he was tempting a puppy with a Good Boy choccy drop.

'Are you still speaking to me, babes? Or have I given you a heart attack?' Now his voice deepened.

'Want me to break down your door and do a bit of mouth to mouth. Claudiaaaaa! Talk to me, babes. If your pop comes home and finds me outside your bedroom he'll castrate me –'

Stefan's patter was irresistible. Plus his chuckle. Not to mention him *babes*-ing me. Suggesting mouth to mouth . . .

On the off-chance his mouth-to-mouth offer was serious, I unfroze from the horror-stricken pose I'd assumed since locking myself in my room. That's where

I'd clocked, in the mirror behind my door, the unabridged horror of what Stefan had already clocked. *Mamma Mia!* It wasn't a pretty sight. So before his reason recovered from the shock and he ran screaming from our house, I threw on Dad's shirt over my jeans.

'Now that's a look. We'll be Macho-girl and Babyface.' Stefan stepped right into my room as soon as I opened up. The tips of his fingers caught mine and before I could breathe he pulled me against him. Then he kissed me, his mouth soft, but it's pressure hard enough to graze my lips with my teeth.

Holy Moley! I didn't know people's leg muscles stopped working when they were snogged.

Must be why you always see couples clutching on to each other for dear life in the movies or doing fumbly business lying down. It's not to make the experience more sexy at all. It's just snoggers being plain sensible. *(Note to self: Ask Georgina in my next email why the hell she didn't warn me about any of this.)*

For my first smooch, only Stefan's fingertips kept all ten and three-quarter stone of me upright, so when my legs gave way, I ended up toppling forward. Biting down on Stefan's tongue before headbutting him in the crotch on my slip to the floor. I was mortified, but Stefan just dabbed his mouth and laughed.

'Babes, how did you know bringing people to their knees turns me on?' He was still laughing while he grabbed my wrists. Tugged me upright. 'Better not do that again without warning. I might just fight back. Come on.'

Keeping hold of me with one hand, Stefan tried to lead me downstairs.

'Shoes. Socks,' I said, pulling against him.

'Don't need them. I've wheels outside.'

'Need shoes though –'

Stefan answered by pulling me harder.

'I'll carry you to my car, babes –'

'D'you want a hernia? What's the rush?'

I was giggling. Breathless. Stefan was running downstairs now, me in tow.

'Quick, 'fore the cops come back. Wreck our date.'

He'd the front door open before I managed to twist myself out of his grip. 'Cool the beans. Need my key. Need to leave my dad a note. Oh and hang on –' I started quick-checking the kitchen worktops, the hall table where all the mail piled up, buzzing from the family room to the coat-stand by the front door, patting all Dad's pockets. 'My dad's missing his VISA. Need to have a shifty –'

My search can't have taken up more than a minute but Stefan seemed mightily impatient about having to hang about. He stayed by the front door, tapping his boot on the floor, checking his mobile. The donk one tonight. When I scooted past him to go upstairs he grabbed my arm.

'Hey, where you off to now?'

'Dad's room.'

Stefan grinned at me. Didn't let go my arm though.

'Didn't spot any free credit while I was in there –'

'Look. I'll be up and down.' I tried to release myself. Couldn't.

'Babes, it's safer cancelling the card. Then it doesn't matter if it's missing.'

'How?'

Stefan's phone donked: ***Another One Bites The*** . . .

'Use an old statement,' he said as he was putting the

mobile to his ear. He let my arm go so he could flap me away with his hand.

'Later. Soon. Not yet,' Stefan said into the phone without waiting to hear who was calling. He followed me through the hall, stopping at Dad's filing cabinet under the stairs. 'Bet you'll find your old man's card details in here with all his bills, babes,' he said like he could see through metal. While I flipped obediently through a drawer, Stefan leaned his elbows on the top of the cabinet.

'Just thinking –' he said while I was thinking how much I loved the way he stroked his fingertips over the top of my hand before he took the VISA statement I pulled out '– I better talk to VISA instead of you. Kid on I'm the cardholder. If *you* say it's your dad's account . . . Y'know. Gorgeous girl's voice . . . Man's name on the card . . .' He shrugged.

I rolled my eyes.

'Course. They'd want to speak to Dad. Not me. Just as well you're here. Think we need to cancel? I mean the card's probably –'

I circled my arm about the kitchen till Stefan

waggled his finger at me. 'Better safe than sorry. Some crook could be going wild with your dad's plastic and we're standing here talking about it –'

He'd our kitchen phone. Dad's statement in his hand. Already reading the Lost or Stolen card number on it. Dialling.

'Don't happen to know your dad's PIN number or password? Your mum's maiden name?' he covered the mouthpiece and whispered. 'Case they take me through security. Won't tell a soul.'

Stefan was crossing his heart with his finger when his call was answered. When I wrote down CLODDY and the year I was born on a piece of paper for him, he took my pen to draw a massive love-heart round them.

11 stefan's crib

'Surprised I'd to give stuff from your dad's passwords,' Stefan said when Dad's VISA was sorted. 'Lucky you knew them. It's usually star signs they ask for.'

'M'dad uses the same code for everything,' I shrugged.

'Does he now? Keeps all his eggs in one basket. Very handy.' Stefan chuckled. Then blew me a kiss across the palm of his hand.

'Catch, babes. Quick,' he said.

I chuckled back.

Finally, officially, were on our second date. Whoopee! I'd even managed to get myself into socks and shoes while Stefan was busy talking with VISA downstairs. And I'd combed my hair. Brushed the Artex off the roof of my mouth and had a gargle with Listerine.

Now we were in Stefan's car. A dinky two-seater I could barely fold my great big self inside. Not much roomier than the toy models Dad used to buy Neil, it was low-slung and going like stink. Even when Stefan passed a REDUCE SPEED sign, and vroomed through a 20s PLENTY zone avenued with luxury flats, it was going like stink.

So fast I wished Stefan's left hand stayed on the wheel and not my knee, much as I enjoyed the thrill of his touch.

So fast my heart filled my mouth so I said zilch on the journey.

Didn't even ask how come a young guy like Stefan was running round in a motor like this. No.

Or how come, when Stefan parked the car alongside a hulking black jeepy thing inside a private basement garage in the newest block of the luxury flats we'd just boy-racered past, he pressed 'Penthouse' when we were in the lift.

Too fast. That was too fast for me. This is too fast for me, was all I could think while a glass lift slicked me from underground to cloud level. Silly me forgot to take my stomach on board as hand luggage.

'Oh Jeez Louise.'

With nothing to hold on to I made a grab for the lapels of Stefan's leather coat, but his hands blocked mine and he seized my wrist. Pulled me against him.

'Don't you like getting high, Claudia?' his lips brushed my earlobe as he whispered and I thought my legs might go again.

Kiss me again and say my name. Please, I prayed, closing my eyes, tilting my chin up hopefully and swaying a little against the soft cool of Stefan's coat. But there was no more snogging, alas and alack. Instead, the lift gave a trendy-sounding ping and Stefan, holding me at arm's length, walked me backwards.

'Welcome to my humble abode,' he intoned.

God love him, he might be gorgeous but he was *definitely* one of those guys who shouldn't do funny accents. I think he thought he sounded Transylvanian. Just sounded Welsh.

Although, cheek of me to slag Stefan's voice. I couldn't even make mine work. Not when I took in the crib Stefan had himself.

I'm not exaggerating. I'd never even seen anything as posh in a *mag,* let alone for real.

My jaw practically hit Stefan's pale wooden floor while I gawped from his white leather sofas with their snow-fluff cushions to the unsmudged stainless steel of his galley kitchen. Blinked at the walls made entirely of window. Beyond them twinkled the panorama of Glasgow by night where car lights glittered like ruby or diamond strings snaking through blue-black darkness.

'It's beautiful. But where d'you get the wonga for this? And how d'you keep it so tidy?' I gasped. And OK, it was better than: *Are you sure you're not actually gay?* but still out of line. So I backtracked. Frantically. 'S'just that. Y'know. You're young and . . . well aren't you a student or something . . .'

My babble petered into silence. I looked at Stefan, but he was pushing buttons on a keypad that I thought was an abstract painting. That moany droney *My Funny Valentine* song I bloody *detest* filled the space between us.

'S'just . . . What's your . . .? Are you . . .? You've not said . . .'

'You've not asked, babes.'

Stefan had moved to his kitchen area. He was taking things from a fridge that was bigger than our back garden: out came salads covered in cling film stamped with the name of the swankiest deli in Glasgow. Likewise a cheese platter. Dips. Dishes of olives and hummus. The sight was enough to trigger a howl from my belly loud enough to drown Stefan's horrible choice of music. My hangover had cost me a day's worth in time and food.

'OK then, I'm asking now. Are you a student?' I had to boost my voice to mask the volcanic activity in my gut.

'Sort of.' Stefan was uncorking a bottle of white wine.

'Cool. What'ya studying?'

Stefan shrugged. Turned his back to me, fiddling in a cupboard full of glasses. He handed me a crystal flute of wine before chink, chink, chinking ice into a second glass then filling it with water from one of those fancy fridge dispensers we don't have in our kitchen.

(Note to self: Maybe I should try for uni instead of the police. Student loans must buy you more than I thought.)

'What am I studying? Chemistry, I suppose.' Stefan joined me on his white leather. 'I'm interested in compounds. And business.'

'How d'you mean you "suppose" you're doing chemistry? What year are you? What uni? And aren't you having wine?'

'Questions, questions. I'll answer the most important one: good boys like me don't drink and drive.'

Stefan clinked his glass to mine. Leaned in to rub my nose with his. 'FYI,' he went on, 'I'm a part-time student right now. Kinda getting sidelined into the family business more and more. Helping out –'

'So you work?' I cut in, 'Aha. S'that how you afford this place? I mean –'

'Whoa, babes. My turn for a question.'

Stefan put his arm round my shoulders, pulling me nearer him.

'Why the inquisition? Are you a reporter? Or a police officer?'

'That's three questions. And how can I be a cop if I'm still at St Bloody Mary's school taking resits I'm going to fail. Supposed to be studying right this minute actually –'

I sipped at my wine, wishing, to be honest, that I could be drinking Stefan's iced-water instead. Or better still, a nice big cuppa. Four sugars. I decided I must still be hungover, because the wine left a nasty, sour taste in my mouth. Every time I swallowed, my throat burned. Made me burp. Feel really queasy.

'Sorry,' I covered my mouth. 'Don't usually drink much.' I was moving to put my glass on Stefan's coffee table, but he stayed my hand.

'Try a few more sips, babes. You're drinking a Sancerre. Very dry. Bit of an acquired taste if you're more used to alcopops.'

Cheek, I was ready to say. *Last night you accused me of being a Burger King girl. Now this. I'm a cider girl, me,* but Stefan was tipping the rim of my goblet up. Holding it to my mouth.

'Mmmm.'

Three or four forced glugs later I zipped my lips. Pushed the glass away.

'Look, can I just have water? I don't like your fancy wine.' *Or the way you're pouring it down my throat, pal.*

I must have sounded sharp when I hauled myself off the sofa next to Stefan and thumped into the one opposite. To be honest I was actually going for the breadsticks he'd laid out but he must have thought he'd upset me. Over he came. Dropped to his knees.

'Babes, I'm being a jerk. See. Me and girls. I'm not used to entertaining or . . . Look. Can we start again?'

Stefan's eyes were wide and worried. When he brushed his hair from his face and smiled, he looked so baby-faced and sweet and drop-dead gorgeous I couldn't . . . Well, first of all, I couldn't believe he wasn't a player with *real* babes . . . just *didn't* buy there being no other females fighting each other for a piece of him.

So why me? I asked myself, not for the first time in the last two days. *Do you really, actually fancy me? Or are you messing? What's your game, matey?*

But when I looked into Stefan's eyes, I couldn't have cared less what his game was.

I just wanted to put my arms round him.

'Course we can start again. So how about another of those kisses now that I'm sitting down.'

Unfortunately, since I'd breadsticks covered with hummus in both hands and two cheekfuls of olives, I had to console both myself and Stefan with soothing grunts till my mouth was empty. By which time he was back in his kitchen. I watched him footer with his designer kettle like he'd never worked one before.

'How long you been here?' I yawned, settling myself more comfortably into the leather sofa. Don't think I'd ever parked myself in anything so soft. And the room was on the warm side. I could have slept if I closed my eyes.

Still paying for going over the score last night, my eyes weighed heavier and heavier as I watched Stefan open and shut cupboards. Funny. Like my dad, he didn't seem to know where anything was in his own kitchen.

'How long?' Stefan was putting a couple of mugs on a tray. 'Well, we've only had this place a few weeks.'

'We?' I heard myself ask through another yawn. *Knew it. He lives with someone. Some size zero model* . . . I sighed in my head, yet weirdly I felt too relaxed and comfy to let the thought upset me. Anyway, before it could, Stefan said, 'Me and my dad and my uncle own it.'

'Your dad?' I yawned again, my voice sounding faraway. Slurred too.

'He livezere? Zee coming back?'

'Not tonight, babes. Just relax.'

Stefan set down a tray of mugs and tea on his coffee table. Then he knelt in front of me again. Began to prop me up with all the cushions scattered over his sofa.

'Just you and me,' he whispered, running his hand over my hair. 'All night long. Dad's usually abroad. I run his businesses here –'

'Biznizizzzz?' I could barely move my mouth. *Can't stay here all night,* I wanted to say, but I couldn't seem to form the words.

'Pharmaceuticals. Export and distribution. Kinda complicated to describe –'

'Mmmm,' I felt myself nodding in slow motion. 'Zat why you do chemistry then?' I dragged words from my head, the muscles round my mouth like lead when I tried to speak. 'So whered'youztudy . . .?'

'So what's all muddy, babes? Hey, you're so tired. Definitely too many cocktails last night. Shhhhh now . . .'

Stefan was busy tucking a furry white throw round me now. Round my shoulders, down my arms, my hips, under my legs. The push of his fingertips through the fabric triggered a memory of Mum's bedtime touch when I was small. How safe her nearness used to make me feel. Loved. Protected . . .

But tonight Mum doesn't know where I am. She's on the other side of the world and I'm in some guy's flat. And I'm feeling really strange . . .

That was the moment I tried to gee myself. Move. Kick off the throw. Push Stefan's hands from my thighs. They were hot and heavy and strong. Pressing down. Holding me still. Though I wasn't entirely sure. His face was close to me and again I thought, though *again* I wasn't entirely sure because everything inside my head was so foggy, that he was asking me something about seeing those hammer guys outside Dad's shop again.

'Did you babes? Would you know them? Tell *me* the truth –' but I couldn't focus on his words.

'Get off, will you?' I do remember grunting that. Willing my body to work. Screaming at myself inside my head:

Get up, Claudia! Stay awake! Don't just slump there like a big sack of spuds.

But, for the second time in Stefan's company – embarrassing coincidence or what? – I was completely paralysed. Like in those dreams I've had where I need to fight or run but my body lets me down.

I'm alone with some guy I hardly know, I realised when cold needles of panic pricked my wooziness. *No address left for Dad on the kitchen table.* Just:

> Guess what? Gone out 6-ish. Hot
> date for Cloddy! C u 18r pa x

How much older and more stupid did I need to become before I found myself in a major pickle? I mean Stefan seemed perfectly safe. In fact he seemed perfect. But I'd known him little over a day and right now he was in a position to do *anything* to me: Kill me. Torture me.

Worse: he could rape me. I couldn't stop him. Couldn't even stay conscious.

failed getaway

Something was snorty-growling very close to me. The sound rose and fell, ugly and slobbery and wet. Like something you might hear from a rhinoceros with a heavy cold. It was loud. Very. Jarring with the tinny niggle of *I Am the Walrus* nearby. When I groaned the growling stopped. Which meant – oh dear, and oh how mortifying – I'd been snoring again.

Properly awake now, I tried to stand. Couldn't. I was swaddled in blankets, head bricked in with stacks of cushions and pillows. *What's happened to me? Where am I? What time is it?* I groped for thoughts, my head even duller than it had been after all that champagne I'd drunk the other night. *And those cocktails that had wiped my memory.* No headache though. No queasiness either, thank goodness. Just muddy thoughts and a big worrying blankness between the last things I could remember and now.

Stefan. Hot hands. Heavy limbs. Questions. Sleep. Fear . . .

I could grasp at these details but couldn't sharpen them beyond blurry in my memory. I shook my head. No use. Everything was still fuzzy, apart from the high-pitched notes of my phone. Still ringing. Close enough to my ear that I felt it vibrate. Stopping before I could grope about for it. Then ringing again.

'Babes. Thank goodness! You're back in the land of the living. I've phoned you non-stop. What happened last night? You *totally* crashed on me. Some of us have done a day's work while you've been snoring. And by the way, do you *snore* –'

Stefan's voice was bright. Full of laughter.

'Snoring? Me?' My own voice was raspy. Small.

'Kidd-ing, My Sleeping Beauty, you were.'

Stefan clicked his tongue to dismiss the worry in my voice. He sounded anxious when he spoke again. 'You still with me, babes? You OK? I'm coming over.'

'No. Need to get home.' I was on my feet now. Still

fully dressed, by the way. Apart from my shoes which were paired and waiting for me on a little mat at the end of the sofa.

Thank God. He didn't . . . I've not been . . . I'm still . . . I shook away the thoughts I was having, guilty I was even having them now, especially with Stefan on the end of the phone. So pleased to hear me. Friendly. Caring.

How could I have doubted this guy's intentions?

'Listen,' I told him. 'M'dad doesn't know where I – haven't seen him for a whole day and – oh no, it's Monday. I've school. What time is it?'

'Claudia. Claudia. You need to relax more, babes –' Stefan's chuckle interrupted me.

'You've no school today. Not with an upset stomach. It's sorted. I phoned you in sick. St Mary's, yeah?'

'But I'm not –' Stefan wasn't letting me speak.

'You've to get well soon. "Tell her to take a couple of days, Mr Quinn," that's what your dame in the office said, so you don't need to show up till midweek. Just hang out. My place is your place –'

'But I can't. My dad – I need to . . .?'

'You texted him last night, babes. He's sorted too.'

'No I didn't –'

'He thinks you did.'

'Huh?'

'You told him you went to Fran's to study history –'

'I didn't. Fran's not even in my history class.'

Never was. What's more she wasn't even at school any more; worked as a teller in the Royal Bank. I tried to tell Stefan but he was assuring me, 'You told pops you were with her.'

'No. I left him a note about going on a date. He'll worry sick about me. He'll have the police out –'

'But you sent him a text when your date stood you up. "Dumped. Boohoo. Surprise, surprise. Revising with Fran instead. Staying over."'

'I didn't say *that,*' I said. Winced: why did Stefan *have* to have said *surprise, surprise*? I was sharper with him when I asked, 'And how d'you know who Fran is –?'

'And how did I get her number? And how did I unlock your phone to read through your address book? Your texts. Find a chum you could be kipping over with?'

In the silence on the line I heard myself breathing hard.

How did you? That's private stuff.

'Tried those Quinn passwords, didn't I? Remember you gave them to me last night? Handy that. Hey, just as well you can trust me with your secrets.' Stefan's voice was low. A murmur. 'Not just a pretty baby-face, am I ?' he added, and when he spoke, I'd the eensiest suspicion a second voice guffawed some remark to Stefan in the background.

'Where are you?' I sounded snappy.

'On my way to you, babes,' Stefan replied, adding, 'Hey, your dad texted back, last night, by the way. He's been a very naughty boy.'

Phew, I thought when I checked my Inbox. Dad had bought the Fran lie. Why wouldn't he, anyway? Sad girls like me don't get up to the things that worry parents. Never have the opportunity.

Work hard

Dad's text began.

Sorry your date dissied you.
Bloke's loss. Who was this
joker anyway?

It went on. And on. Dad's one of these pedantic technophobes who texts in full words:

Done for speeding on A9
yesterday. Twice. Six points.
No driving licence in wallet.
Can you look for that now, else
I'll be charged? Still no VISA???
See you tonight, Cloddy. Yer Pa
xx ps Polis want to talk to you
again – 'urgent'. Better stay on
their good side for the sake of
my driving record.

I clicked REPLY to let Dad know I'd cancelled his VISA, but when I saw my battery was almost flatlining I decided to head home instead. Look for his licence. See what the cops wanted. The walk would clear my head. So I checked through my address book for Stefan's number, having a dander through his flat while it rang out. It was a strange crib altogether. Every drawer, every wardrobe and every cupboard was empty. New smelling. Unused. And everything was white. Except Stefan's bathroom which was white and chrome with a silvery rubber floor.

'A wet-room. Wow. Mum's fantasy,' I whispered peeking into a couple of bedrooms so pristine, I couldn't believe anyone had ever slept in the identically made-up beds.

Doesn't look like Stefan even stayed here last night, I thought, as his phone clicked from ringing out to voicemail.

Definitely Stefan's voicemail. Although I didn't have a clue what his message was instructing me. You see, I recognised Stefan's voice all right. And his name when he pronounced it. But not the language he was speaking. No. It was Double Dutch as far as I was concerned.

Oh. Apart from one word.

If I'm ever in a pub quiz or on 'Millionaire' and I'm asked the Double Dutch term for psychopath, I'll be able to say, 'It's *psychopath,* Chris. Final answer.'

doubting stefan

Do you ever get something into your head about someone? Like they're out to stab you in the back even though they're being sweeter than a Caramac to your face?

Funnily enough, Fran, my supposed swot-mate, was a bit like that with me. Strange that out of all the names in my phone (about six if I have to be honest) Stefan should have picked her: The Girl Least Likely to Invite Clod Quinn for a Sleepover. Ever.

She was only *in* my phone at all because she'd asked Georgina for my number to send me a text-slag during games last year.

Don't trip, Bigfoot.

She used to call me that. Or 'Plod', on account of my size nines. So I'd stored her number to tb. When I finally thought of something suitably insulting.

> Does counting beans all day
> hurt your brain?

was the best I'd come up with, so I was biding my time.

But maybe Stefan picking Fran's name at random from my address book's a sign. That I should watch myself . . .

I'd planted these doubts into my head about Stefan in the moments between hearing his Double Dutch phone message and trying to get his lift door to open.

See it wouldn't.

'There's no button. I'm trapped.' I worked myself into an instant lather, banging and kicking at the lift, even shouting 'Help Me. I'm kidnapped,' a couple of times. Honestly, I must have watched *Panic Room* too many times, because even while I was shouting blue murder I was opening Stefan's unlocked front door. The door faced a stairwell. Duh! A helpful green running man on the wall was pointing down it beneath the flashing words WAY OUT.

Eleven floors later and with thighs like solid rubber,

I ran out of steps to descend. I'd to pause on the tiny landing, hands on knees catching my breath before shoving down the emergency-bar on the one-way metal door in front of me. Expecting a rush of fresh air and rain on my face I was thrown, not only to find myself in darkness, but to smack hard into something cold and metal.

A car. Stefan's dinky sports car, I presumed.

'Oooyah,' I rubbed my shin where I'd grazed it on Stefan's number-plate. Then felt my way round the vehicle's soft top, hand over hand. How the hell did I get out now? And if Stefan's car was here, where was he?

The garage was completely sealed to daylight, only a dim strip of sickly green from the stairwell breaking the pitch darkness. *And I can't get back out that way, either,* I thought as I began groping my way along the walls. I was feeling for a light switch, hearing my own breath coming in short grunts.

'I saw fine last night when we drove in. There must be lights,' I spoke aloud, trying to keep myself together. But any section of wall I ran my hand along was smooth. And there were no obvious buttons round the facing of Stefan's huge metal up-and-over garage door. No handle on the inside either.

I'd have to wait for Stefan now.

'Buggeritis!' my voiced bounced back to me off the concrete walls. More in frustration than hope, I turned and whumped my backside against the garage door. No movement, just a rippling metallic clang. I whumped again. Ouch! Harder. And what do you know? This second time, the door yielded.

'We're out of here, Big Butt,' I congratulated myself, jerking my hips forwards and then whamming my backside back for what I hoped might be the third and final push.

Except there was no door to butt this time. No. Soundlessly it had slid open and now hung above me, leaving my great battleship of an arse greeting the passengers of a big black jeepy motor driving at speed down the garage ramp.

rings on his fingers

One of the front seat passengers in the jeepy motor was Stefan. When its brakes slammed on and it skidded to a stop about a hair's breadth from my left buttock, he leapt out of it although I didn't recognise him immediately. He was wearing a pinstriped suit smarter than anything Dad had ever worn for work. No sign of the Man in Black coat he'd on last night. No black jeans. No cowboy boots.

So where d'you change gear? I would have asked if Stefan hadn't been barking out something which included my name into the jeepy car as he slammed its passenger door and made flappy Get Away signals to the driver. I couldn't make out who Stefan gestured at. The face behind the wheel was totally invisible thanks to the charcoal privacy glass you get in fancy cars; but as soon as Stefan waved, his driving companion ground into reverse with a crunching desperation that even a fledgling driver like myself knew ain't healthy for any gearbox. Far too quickly for me to peer through the windscreen to check out this nutter on the clutch, the jeepy wheelspinned. Never even entered the garage.

'What was all that about?' I watched the jeepy's shrinking tail lights, my hands wafting through a filthy belch of exhaust smoke. Its bitterness in my nostrils combined with thc sour tang of burnt rubber on tarmac. 'What's Mikey's hurry?' I spluttered.

'Mikey, babes?' Glancing quickly from me to where the jeepy should have been if its driver had stuck to the speed limit for a residential area, Stefan frowned at me.

'Mikey Schumacher. Y'know: racing driver? That guy's driving like him. And what's with the suit?' I started to say, but Stefan silenced me by stretching his arm across my chest. With gentle pressure he backed me into the garage. His voice seemed tight, like he was annoyed but trying to hold back from showing it.

'What the hell are you doing down here, babes? Nearly got flattened. You weren't leaving without telling me?' he said, with a dry laugh, and before I knew what was happening, or could decide what

Stefan really thought about my failed getaway, the massive metal door I stupidly thought I'd opened with my magic bum lowered like a well-oiled drawbridge. The garage was in darkness again.

'Hey, hang on –'

Now I was the one sounding strained, my voice bouncing off concrete walls like stretched elastic. 'Look, I need to head. I was down here trying to find a way out –'

'Babes, what's Mikey's hurry?'

Stefan's voice sounded back to normal, his tone soothing, not strained or stern any more. I felt his palm cupping the back of my head. When he echoed the question I'd asked him about the jeepy's driver, mimicking my sarkiness, his breath was a warm chuckle in my ear. The sudden nearness of him sent a shiver through me and I let him take my hands and lead me further into the pitch dark of the garage, even though I didn't like it in there. I liked it even less when he twirled me under his arm like we were dancing in the dark and I lost my bearings. Couldn't tell if Stefan was in front of me, behind me, still with me for that matter.

'Hey! Where are you?' I was bleating. Groping my arms about. 'Switch a light on, will you? Coz I really need to go now . . .'

Instead of Stefan's voice, silence rang back.

'Stefan?'

Silence still.

'Look,' now my voice was cracking. Gulpy. 'This isn't funny. Let me see to get out.'

Silence again. Enough already.

'You're being a bastard,' I hissed, and instead of feeling scared any more, a surge of anger wiped my uneasiness. Sticking my arms in front of me, I stomped a few zombie steps forwards until my hands met metal.

At the garage door I bunched my fists and began to pummel.

'Someone let me out of –' I took a deep breath and hollered, but before I could get anywhere near the volume I was aiming for, my wrists were grabbed. I was birled round and grasped tight.

'Babes,' Stefan soothed, squashing my cheek against his pinstripes. 'I had to punish you for running out on me. You mustn't do things like that –' Stefan's mouth was in my hair while he spoke, his voice a whisper, 'Because we're not done yet. Oh no, no, no . . .'

When Stefan shoved me up against the garage door, the back of my skull clonked the metal hard enough to send a ripple through it that made my teeth vibrate. The impact wasn't sore exactly, but it wasn't pleasant. Stefan wasn't being nearly as gentle as he looked . . .

I don't know whether to be scared or excited, I realised, deciding, *actually, I'm both: kinda turned on by a guy who likes rough.*

Stefan had my upper arms pinned against my sides in the vice-grip of his hands. When he ground his mouth against mine in a flat, closed-lip kiss, I tasted my own blood.

'Get into my car now, babes,' Stefan muttered, his lips still pressed to mine. Then he let me go. Reaching above my head he flicked a switch. Bright, yellow light exploded the darkness away.

I was so dazzled I had to cover my face. Black floaters bopped about beneath my eyelids while my vision tried to adapt to the strip-lights. At first, the floaters moved formlessly; sea-monkey-sized dots behind my fingers like interference on a telly with the brightness too high. But just before I took my hands away and opened my eyes properly, something very strange happened. The floaters started to move together, gathering to combine into a single image. Now all this happened in the space of . . . oh, no more than a couple of seconds, and I didn't have a clue how this bizarre still came to be stored in my head like a mental photo I couldn't recall taking. I mean if I could have chosen a pin-up for my Subconscious Mind, I'd've had Stefan's smiling babyface pixelated to the inside of my eyelids, or maybe Johnny Depp in his Captain Jack Sparrow get-up.

Certainly something sexier and less chav than two gold-ringed hands gripping a steering wheel. But that was the picture that flashed up in my head when the floaters stopped floating: a pair of ugly sovereign-bedecked hands, complete with tattooed letters inked across their kunckles. How tacky! Quickly I closed my eyes, shaking my head to clear away the image. The steering wheel faded immediately. But not the fingers. That was really weird. They hung in my mind's eye, their middle joints showing white as if they were gripping on to something. Pulling it . . .

Stefan was opening the passenger door of his car for me – 'Hop in, babes' – when I remembered what these fingers reminded me of, and where I'd seen them before.

'Make yourself comfortable.' Stefan clicked his tongue the way you catch the attention of a pet dog when you want it to obey. I did, slipping my low-slung backside on to the low-slung seat beside Stefan like a zombie. All I could think about was how the ringed hands of whoever had driven Stefan into his garage five minutes ago gripped a steering wheel exactly like I'd seen a hairline gripped two days earlier. Roughly. Cruelly. Before these fingers had pulled back a man's head. Slamming it into . . .

Nah. Behave yourself, Claudia. You're getting one of those flashbacks about the hammer attack. Just like Stefan said might happen . . . I decided, on the brink of blurting out how Stefan was right about his subconscious mind theory: I *had* seen something useful I could tell Starsky and Hutch. *And hey, what a coincidence: the driver of the jeepy that's just left made me remember something about one of those bampots outside Dad's shop . . .*

But the echoey roar of Stefan's engine, accelerating from the gloom of the underground garage into the sunshine of a Monday no-school morning, drowned anything I could have said. Left me blinking my head clear of everything but daylight.

Besides which, Stefan had his music blaring . . . Actually, deary me, it wasn't music. It was Westlife. One of their heinous ballads about flying or wings or soaring roses or something: drivel. Though from the look on Stefan's face as he sang along I could see he was right into it. Word perfect, totally flat, he belted out the lyric like Ray Charles himself was speaking to his soul.

'Isn't this amazing, babes?' Stefan interrupted himself just before that essential and completely gut-turning chord change section you have in every boyband slow number where the pretty laddios get cheered for standing up off their stools in synch without falling over.

'What's amazing? That CD? I think it's a pile of –' Slunk down in the passenger seat in case anyone I knew saw me and thought this was my kind of muzac too, I was about to let rip about the crapness of soppy pop but Stefan pressed a button on his dashboard that made the car roof bzzz open up. He flung his arm around my shoulder and took his eyes off the road to smack a kiss on my cheek.

'Everything!' he shouted, putting his foot down to accelerate on to the Clydeside Expressway.

'You and me, babes –'

Stefan drove too fast for either of us to hear another note or word over the roar of his engine, although I did try to shout he'd been flashed by a speed camera so maybe he should slow down. But my stupid hair kept blowing into my mouth whenever I opened it. Made it impossible to talk. During the journey I couldn't ask where Stefan had been during the night while I thought he was in the flat with me.

How come he'd changed his clothes.

And I couldn't ask him about the Double Dutch message on his mobile.

Who exactly was the guy with the rings in the jeepy?

And why had this same guy zoomed away so fast?

But I knew all these questions, not to mention what

really happened on my First Date, should be asked. And answered. *Before you hang about with this Stefan fella any longer*. That's what Mum and Dad and Georgina would be advising.

All of them right too. *So I'm definitely going to grill Stefan over breakfast.*

That's what I instructed myself at the start of our ride into town.

But ten minutes later, when Stefan pulled up and parked on a double yellow outside Strut, the most expensive clothes shop in Glasgow, I could barely remember my own name let alone the topics I needed to discuss with my mystery date. Talk about blowing away the cobwebs? I think Stefan's driving blew my sense out the back of my head.

Far too fast. Crazy. Not even funny crazy. This guy's reckless – I was aware of a breathless voice of reason niggling at me as Stefan came round to my passenger door and opened it. But I was too windswept to do anything but take his hand and let him steer my wobbly legs to the threshold of a non-Clod world.

15

personal shopping

Strut was one of those shops with a bell outside. Not exactly Glasgow, that.

'Needs to get over itself,' Georgina – who only ever bought clothes from One World or Save the Children – used to say whenever we passed it. One Saturday afternoon we swanned up and rang Strut's bell. No one let us in, although this arseless, spray-tanned blonde sneered out at us both as if she was Glaswegian aristocracy and me and Georgina were turds in matching Fair Trade T-shirts

'Torn-faced tart,' Georgina had opined in her debating club voice as the Torn-Faced Tart turned her back to attend to some essential folding. When Georgina pressed the bell again, keeping her finger on it this time, the TFT swanned over to the door and flipped the sign on it to CLOSED. Me and Georgina had mooned her then.

I wonder if she recognises me, I gulped when same blonde was flipping the CLOSED sign on me again. This however was once I was *inside* Strut. And after she'd greeted Stefan with a triple kiss and not a glance in my direction.

'Hi-yaaa. So fant*a*stic to see you. Your Versace just looks *great* on you,' she shrilled at him in this Lorraine Kelly-esque voice that soooo didn't match the filthy head-to-toe dart of scorn she threw me when Stefan said, 'This is Clau–'

'Listen: Oh. My. God, Stephen,' without bothering to catch my name this shop assistant lunged for Stefan's arm, whirlwinding him through the shop. Although I couldn't see another soul in the place, she was gushing at him in a secretive whisper.

'I know you spent a fortune last week but I'm telling you, Stephen, these shirts that've just come in, I am *not* joking: you have to check them out and you'll want one in every colour because see with your white suit? They're just *so* made for it and, I swear to God, you'll be the only guy in Scotland wearing one coz they're straight off the catwalk in Milan. Quick, quick –'

Still just in the shop and no more, I watched this no-longer-quite-so-torn-faced stick insect hoiking Stefan through to men's clothing as if all these shirts she was raving about were ready to fly back to Milan without him. She seemed to know Stefan better than I did, *Though why d'you keep calling him Stephen, you snooty bint?* I wondered while I stood abandoned near the entrance of the shop. I felt as welcome as a pimple on the tip of Angelina Jolie's nose in the company of the various anorexic mannequins posed around the shop floor, with their cinched-in waists and their pert pointy boobs and their bored, blank faces. Oh dear, they'd be the templates for the clientele Strut expected, I sighed, wandering over to the nearest sparse rail of ladies' clothing. As you do when you're hanging about in normal clothes shops waiting for someone else, I began to browse, checking the price label first, of course. Holy Moley! Every single garment had a triple figure tag, and the prices seemed to rise inversely with the amount of fabric your money bought you.

What a steal, I snorted, examining this bra-top

contraption. Looked like it was run up from one of the Woolworth's hankies I give Dad every Christmas.

POINT. SHOOT. Shoddy red stitching on each bra cup instructed. £425 dangled the price.

'Made of tat,' I spluttered aloud.

When I plucked the hankie bra off the rail and held its tiny triangles of fabric against my substantial boobs I knew I'd have to describe this ridiculous outfit to Georgina in my next email. To make sure I didn't miss out any details I checked around for the nearest mirror and walked towards it. But as soon as I was a few inches from the rail, the stupid bra in my hands started to shrill:

Beeeeeeeeeeeeeeeeeeeeccccp

Muggins hadn't noticed that – unlike Primark – everything in Strut was attached to a wire. I'd remember next time I popped in, all right! That way I might avoid the attentions of this complete **tank** of a security guard who appeared from nowhere. Slammed me to the floor. Bloody hell! I'm no pushover but before I could say 'I was only looking,' he'd my arm racked up my back and his sturdy beam of a knee rammed into my coccyx.

'Please don't move a muscle,' this bloke requested, squeezing my throat till my eyes bulged. 'Otherwise I'll have to hurt you.'

The white-hot fury in my own squashed voice probably surprised me more than it did the guy spread-eagled across me.

'Comedian. I'll hurt *you* if you don't get off me. I said GET OFF!'

Adrenalin surged through me, pumping up my volume, filling me with fight. Every last stone of me heaved against the security guard as I put into practice the dying-fish-on-a-deck wriggle-move good old ex-wrestler Uncle Super Mike had taught with the guarantee that it would always see me out of trouble if I was jumped. Unfortunately, and despite a snapping back-thrust with my head catching the guard a cracker to his nose – blood everywhere – my grunted efforts were essentially as sorry as a dying fish. I'd met my match. Just couldn't throw this big guy off. Still, my panted unladylike war-cry of, 'Bloody let me up, ya dope. I wouldn't thieve this crap if you paid me,' was loud enough to bring a topless Stefan to the rescue.

'Babes? Problem?'

Stefan's response wasn't exactly a textbook damsel rescue. He didn't even lay a finger on the bloke who'd laid into me: *How dare you assault my lady-friend, you bounder!* However, he didn't seem to need to get physical.

'Oi! Have you a deathwish, pal?' Stefan enquired of the security guard. Not even loudly. And by the time I was free and exhaling and scrabbling to my feet, the tank who'd flattened me was up against the nearest wall looking like he wanted to be molecularly absorbed into it. There was blood pumping out his nose, down his chin.

Give the guy a tissue, I felt like saying to Stefan. He was standing in front of the guard now, just watching him bleed. And as I watched Stefan eyeballing this guy, this snake tattooed across Stefan's bare back watched me. The thickest part of it lay in the space between his jutting shoulder-blades, tail tapering to rest along Stefan's flank, its tip curling up and over his left bicep. The snake's head twisted round on itself so it appeared to be striking outwards. Mouth open, fangs bared, like a toxic warning:

Keep back.

Nice, I winced, wondering why the heck Stefan would want to wear something so vicious underneath his classy designer threads. It wasn't like bodywise he *needed* to embellish anything. His upper torso was preeeeetty buff, all hard, corded muscle, not a spare inch of fat. And his untattooed skin was flawless.

Apart from this ugly great blemish. I wrinkled my nose, watching the snake slither along the skin on Stefan's back, rippling the hump of Stefan's vertebrae when he folded his arms. If the snake hadn't had the same tongue of flame as the little one I'd noticed on Stefan's wrist the day we met, I'd have sworn it was real.

'You blind there, pal?' Stefan tutted at the security guard. 'Not paying attention, then. Because she –' he cocked his head at me as casually as if I was a sack of spuds, 'walked in here with *me*.' *Me* was pronounced particularly low and harsh. Anything but casual, I noticed, watching the security guard's reaction.

Shaven-headed and with a neck on him as thick as me at maths, he was a good four inches taller than Stefan. When Stefan leaned in and spoke to him, his tilted chin was only level with the guard's impressively broad chest. But despite this physical inferiority, Stefan's flat mumble was undiluted menace.

'Look I'm so sorry 'bout this, Mr Josef,' the security guard burbled through a mouthful of blood. He was softly-spoken, his voice a mismatch to his thuggish outward appearance. *And you're not bad-looking either, in a beefed-up, gentle giant way,* I decided.

'I didn't realise you were both . . . and when the alarm went off –' the security guard shrugged, his arm moving from Stefan to me. 'When your friend set off the alarm, I automatically –' He sighed, trying to staunch his nose with the side of his hand. With all the fight out of his shoulders he just looked like a bloke desperate to keep his lousy job.

'Honestly, I can't apologise enough,' this time the security guard spoke to me. 'And I hope I didn't hurt you as much as you hurt me –' With a half-smile he made a reaching gesture towards me. His eyes – brown, warm – were brimming with sorry. *And fear,* I sensed. *Of Stefan. A guy he could mince in one hand. Isn't that weird?*

So I tried to clear the air. 'No bother –' I shrugged.

But a slicing motion from Stefan's hand silenced me. 'You're right there: you *can't* apologise enough – what's your name?' Stefan moved in so close I couldn't see the security guard's face any more. Just heard him murmur, 'Dave Griffen,' before Stefan went on, 'Dave Griffen, yeah? Well, Dave Griffen. You *can't* apologise enough. Not now. Not ever. Can he, babes?'

Though Stefan had raised his voice, he didn't turn round immediately. That's why I assumed I was the 'babes' he was talking to.

'But he *has* apologised.' I was half-laughing. 'And I got him good on the nose. So it's OK. Are we having breakfast now?' I went on.

Then I realised Stefan wasn't speaking to me at all. The babes he meant was the spray-tanned shop assistant. I'd been half-aware of her whispering into a phone at the cash desk when Stefan first rushed over to me. Now she was by his side, flicking invisible smuts from the stupid hankie bra that had caused this horrible scene. While I watched her hanging it back on the clothes-rail like it was a priceless work of art, I was tempted to snatch it. Dab it against poor Dave Griffen's nose.

'Stephen, you're so right,' babes-who-wasn't-me gushed. 'I've just told the boss what's happened and he says Strut won't employ security that can't tell criminals from customers. Especially *personal* customers –'

'Like the ones *I* bring in, huh?' Stefan finished the sentence. While he spoke he planted both hands either side of poor Dave Griffen, trapping him against the wall.

'Do you know who I am?' Stefan said.

'*Do* you?' he repeated in the softest voice I'd heard him use yet.

I watched the gulp in Dave Griffen's Adam's apple when he nodded at Stefan.

Or *Mr Josef,* as Dave Griffen was calling him:

'I do, Mr Josef.'

Well maybe you can fill me in, I'd so loved to have freeze-framed this whole nasty scene and whipped Dave Griffen off into one of the changing rooms to ask, because right now this shirtless Mr Stefan/Stephen/Josef whateverhisname was didn't seem *anything* like the sweet-talking guy I'd met in the newsagent's. My fellow-Minstrels fan. The bloke who was *so* upset at what I might have seen outside Dad's shop. Right now Stefan was hard as nails. With a calm, dangerous power to him. Something I'd never seen in anyone who wasn't a hard-man on the telly.

Who are you? I watched Stefan thumb Dave Griffen from his sight. He was telling the ex-security guard, 'Count yourself lucky to be *walking* out this shop. Right, babes? All settled that he's slinging his hook?' Stefan asked the Babes Who Wasn't Me. Though he wasn't really asking her at all. He was telling her. The way Ray Winstone would give an order. Vinnie Jones. Wee hard man Robert Carlyle. Or Robert De Niro, sleepwalking through one of his bad-guy roles.

Babes, nodding at Stefan, flicked an arm towards Dave Griffen in dismissal.

'Oh, no please, Lynne. Gonna give us another chance.'

Instead of moving away, Dave Griffen tried to plead. 'I've worked here two years. No hassles –' he said, addressing me when both Stefan and the shop assistant ignored him.

And, hey, I'd have spoken up for Dave Griffen if Stefan hadn't planked himself in front of the guy again.

'Mate, what don't you understand?' Stefan's voice was low, his tone as warm and friendly as his smile. 'You've assaulted my friend but I'm letting you walk out in one piece. If I were you, I'd split while the going's good.'

Stefan was still smiling when he jabbed his finger at his own face. I had to strain to catch the final advice he gave Dave Griffen. It might have been spoken quietly, but I heard it loud and clear:

'Underneath this babyface of mine beats the heart of a psychopath.'

16

ducking and diving

'Babes, I need coffee. Let's head up to the bistro. We'll shop after.' Before I could catch my breath to blurt: *What was all that about? Why would you call yourself a psychopath?* I was Stefan's babes again. He'd his hands cupping my face, stroking my shoulders, gentle as fur.

'Y'OK? Sorry I'd to play hardball, but that joker was well out of line with you.'

Smiling into my eyes, sweeter than melted marshmallows, Stefan tucked a strand of hair behind my ear, kissing the tip of my nose. Behind him, through Strut's window I could see the ex-security guard hovering out on the pavement. He was rubbing his shaved head, shaking it like he couldn't believe what had just happened. Then he walked away, his big shoulders hunched.

What HAD just happened?! Stefan . . . Stephen?. . .

was becoming one confusing guy to be around: two babes, two names, two phones, two cars, two snake tattoos, and at least two sides to him . . .

I watched him telling his other *babes* we'd be back in a bit.

'*Fantastic.* See you, Stephen,' Lynne simpered from behind the cash desk, where she was taking forever and a day to swaddle a couple of white T-shirts in tissue paper. Duh! You'd think the tops were antique glass like Mum's fancy bottles, not cotton and – as far as I could see – identical to the ones my dad bought in packs of three at T. K. Max.

'Sixty quid each? For vests?' I spluttered when I spotted the tag Lynne-babes was snipping off. 'Someone's having a larff,' I tried to crack a joke. Lighten things up a bit. But Stefan didn't react to my remark. Lynne though, paused the wrapping ritual to blink at me as though I'd left my brain on the pavement.

'They're D&G,' she stroked the T-shirts like they had feelings, 'and complimentary, Stephen. The boss said. To make up for what's just –' Lynne gave the minutest nod in my direction.

'I like *that,*' I couldn't help blurting. 'I get poleaxed by a scrum forward who thinks I'm shoplifting; he apologises but gets the sack; *you* get free gear. Mister, you got life sussed!' I nudged Stefan, hard enough that his hips bumped the cash desk. I didn't think I'd done anything more outrageous than comment on the bleeding obvious, but Lynne gave this little squeak as if someone under the counter had nipped her bony arse. Unless Lynne's mascara was bothering her, or she'd stomach cramp, I'd say her eyes were narrowed with worry as she peeked through her lashes to gauge Stefan's reaction, although if he had been listening to me, he didn't show it.

What's up with your face? I nearly said to Lynne because after what had just happened this designer shopping lark was a bit much for me. I was hungry too and skipping meals always makes me snappy. But I was too bored to give this poor dolled-up lassie some of the lip she deserved. Poor Lynne babes, I felt pity, not anger, while I watched her decorate her daft parcel with coloured Strut Your Stuff stickers. They kept glueing themselves to her Hollywood nails.

Anyway, it wasn't Lynne-babes who *really* wound me up. It was Stefan.

Because just as we were on the staircase up to this 'amazing bistro' that he said was on the next level, 'and sells the world's best muffins. I promise!' his stupid phone donked.

What's going on here, buster? I thought to myself while Stefan wandered to a corner of the shop to talk in private.

And what am I still doing in this up-its-arse shop?

Why didn't I go home last night?

I didn't even stay where Dad thought I was.

And I let this bloke –

Who I've known less than two days

Who's just threatened a decent guy twice his size with violence

Before proclaiming himself a psychopath

Lie for me!

'This isn't me,' I muttered, looking over at Stefan. Still shirtless, one hand in the pocket of his pinstriped trousers, he prowled the far end of the store, yakking non-stop into his phone. I couldn't swear on this, but it didn't sound like he was speaking in English, though when I tried to concentrate and stare and listen harder, the black pupils of his nasty snake tattoo warned me, like eyes in the back of Stefan's head, to keep my distance.

I decided I would.

'I'm off. See myself out,' I told Lynne. Given the heels she'd on she was round the cash desk impressively fast.

'Without telling Stephen?' she whispered, her eyes two frilly saucers of shock. Then her gushy voice rose loud enough for Stefan to catch what she was saying across the shop.

'Why don't I show *you* some clothes? What are you? A sixteen? Stephen says you're needing a trouser suit.'

'News to me.'

Instead of following Lynne, I unsnecked the door.

'I wouldn't go if I was you,' Lynne's anxious heels teetered after me.

'But you're not me. Ta Ta, babes.' I left her catching flies.

17

the big man

If it hadn't been for the traffic warden outside Strut I'd have been on the subway and home before Stefan knew I'd even left him. But, when I saw this woman pulling back Stefan's front windscreen wiper I had to intervene.

'Hang on.' I belted towards Stefan's car, automatically programmed to do what I always do for Mum: save her a fine and earn myself a tenner for the trouble.

'Two secs. The driver's in that shop. I'll get him to move –'

I reached the car just in time to see the warden replacing Stefan's wiper carefully against the windscreen. There was no sign of a ticket.

'Just say thanks, hen. Tell Mr J to park all day if he wants,' the warden winked at me. She was tucking a twenty-quid note into her breast pocket. Whistling cheerfully as she strolled off.

Gobsmacked, I watched till the warden was out of sight. A question was begining to throb in my head like toothache: *Who the hell is this guy?*

'Babes! There you are.'

Stefan's voice in my ear made me start. But not as much as the grip of his hand round my wrist.

'Have to buy you a lead if you keep running away,' he chuckled from inside the shirt he was pulling over his head. 'Please don't leave me, Claudia.' He let me go to put his hand to his heart. 'At least not before breakfast.'

Laughing, he turned me to face him, this time using the hand holding his mobile. From where I stood I could see Lynne watching us from the shop.

She was chewing on one of her fancy nails.

'No. I'm away home.' I pulled free. Moved off, nodding at Stefan's mobile. 'You're busy. Plus,' I cocked my head at the shop as I walked, 'I didn't like that in there.'

Before I'd taken more than a few steps, Stefan blocked me, laying his arms on my shoulders.

'That bear roughing you up was out of order. But I sorted him for you. Didn't I?'

When I shook my head, Stefan sounded surprised.

'Something else bugging you? Was it Lynne?' His expression switched from grinning to grim as he glared back at the shop. When he eyeballed Lynne she ducked from view.

'Did she say something? One call to the boss I'll have her –'

'What? Sacked? Whacked?' I interrupted.

I twisted myself away from Stefan's hands.

'*You* were the problem in there,' I blurted. 'Coming the big man when that security guy was only doing his job. Now can you let me pass?' I said quietly. When Stefan didn't budge I shouldered him out my road.

'Hey. What d'you think *you're* doing?' Stefan tried to block me again. His voice was so mean, so cold, that I sucked my breath in when I dodged him for the second time.

He must have heard my reaction.

'Oh, Claudia.' A different voice belonging to a

different guy altogether spoke.

'Listen to me. Wally here.' He shook his mobile as if to explain. 'Having a very bad day at the office,' he said. Then he leaned in close to me. He sounded sheepish when he went on, 'Plus I was showing off. You're right; I *was* playing the big man to impress. Coz I think you're something else. Can we rewind?'

While he was speaking – and I could hardly *believe* this was happening to me – Stefan dropped to his knees. In front of me. On a public pavement in Glasgow city centre, for God's sake. Clasping his hands he raised them up to me.

'One more chance, babes,' he begged as a passing white van-man yelled from the road, 'You can do better than that, mate.'

'I don't think so,' Stefan said, his pale eyes searching my face. 'Don't walk away,' he begged. 'I'll be a good boy from now on. Promise.'

Now, not being accustomed to hotties prostrating themselves before me, is it such a surprise that I gave Stefan the benefit of the doubt? Besides, he was being so sweet again. Funny. Charming. Cute.

Really, really cute. Mewling like a kitten in a tangle of wool:

'Miao, miao, Claudia.'

Then panting at me – *huh huh huh,* his hands making puppy paws.

When he begged, 'Pretty-please be my babes. I'll have to whine if you don't –' then lifted his head back and yowled like a coyote with bellyache, I gave in.

'Shut up,' I was laughing. 'People are staring. If you stop yodelling and stand up I might –'

'So you're still my babes! You know I'll do *anything* if you're still my babes.' Stefan quit his baby-animal bribery to double-check, 'Will you still be my babes?' and it was then, when I saw how keen to please me he seemed, that I thought: *OK. Let's see if you keep your promises.*

'Get that security guard his job back and I'll think about it,' I said.

'With one phone call.' Stefan shrugged. *Like I'd asked him to do something really trivial,* I thought while he held out his hands to me.

They were soft and warm, his fingers slender in mine.

'Coffee then. Finally,' he said in a businesslike voice once he was on his feet. 'We won't go through the shop again. There's a back way.'

Stefan's fingertips hooked mine, tightening so I wouldn't have been able to wrench free. *Even if I wanted to,* I thought, letting myself be walked round the corner from Strut's main entrance.

'My belly thinks my throat's cut here,' I was just starting to tell Stefan, when both his donk phone and his *Kill Bill* phone drowned me out.

Letting go my hand, he checked both callers, spitting out a word that had to be a curse though I didn't understand it.

''Scuse, babes,' Stefan turned his back on me and walked away muttering instructions into each mobile. His tone was sharp. Angry. When he turned round again he'd a wad of cash in his hand.

'Listen, no rest for the wicked today,' he sighed, peeling a slab of notes from the wad and tucking it into the front pocket of my jeans. 'Buy yourself something hot and if it costs more than I've given you, just tell Lynne to charge it to me,' he nodded towards Strut.

'And take a cab home.' He was already walking backwards, beeping his car open.

'Duty calls. Promise I'll ring.' He crossed his heart. Blew me a kiss.

'See you soon, babes. Promise that too.'

18
all day breakfast

'I'll have scrambled eggs, bacon, mushrooms, couple of sausages, tomatoes and black pudding, thanks.'

'Toast, doll?'

'Just two slices. Actually make it three.'

Well, a big girl like me's gotta eat and I'd win no medal passing out from hunger on the subway home (Take a cab, my eye, sweet-talking guy!). With at least two broken promises on the muffin-and-coffee front from Stefan, and all that good scoff-time wasted faffing about watching T-shirts being pamper-wrapped, I was famished. So famished I was seriously tempted to *eat* the All Day Breakfast menu in the caff I chose to splurge some of Stefan's money in. Just as well it was laminated because I was drooling from the moment I took a seat at the only free table and gave my order.

Stefan can stick his muffins, I thought, wondering how

Georgina and myself had missed this little Paradise of a greasy spoon the day we wasted time mooning poor Lynne-babes.

Soon as my hearty breakfast arrived, I wired in without pausing for breath. Only when my plate was cholesterol-free and my arteries were hardening did I lean back in my chair to nosey the other folk in the caff.

A trendy bistro it wasn't, most of the customers variations of the coffin-dodger brigade who kept my dad in business: old biddies in rain-mates counting out the exact change for their tea and scone, and old geezers in flat caps and greasy anoraks, slurping from mugs. Dropping crumbs over the racing page on their *Daily Record*. The only talking in the caff came sandwiched between raucous bursts of dirty laughter from a crowd of workies in boiler suits and building site boots. These blokes filled a row of tables along one wall, one group standing over another till the first lot and their bacon rolls shifted.

It'd be nice for me to say that some of the fitter workies gave me the eye, given that I was the only female in the caff without a free bus pass or false teeth, but not even the beer-belliest ugliest worky threw me a glance.

Despite this, as I munched on my final slice of toast I felt I was being watched. Eyes on my neck. Someone behind me. And I was right. When I turned in my chair, bringing up an impressive tomato-sauce and eggy burp as I swivelled at the waist, there was this guy sat at the table behind. Staring right at me.

'Hello again,' he smiled. 'You doing all right?'

Honestly. What was I like? I know generations of my teachers over the years have depressed Mum and Dad with variations on the Parent's Night lament that I never pay attention to *anything* and have the memory of a retarded goldfish, but personally I'd never totally bought into the notion that my brain was wired to the moon.

Till the moment this big bloke in the caff moved his chair next to mine and said, 'Listen. I'm really sorry 'bout what happened back there.'

Honestly. I didn't have a *clue* who this bloke was or what he was on about.

Well not instantly. And it wasn't totally my fault. Because Dave Griffen had made identification complicated for big Clod: he'd a woolly hat pulled right down to his eyes and he'd stripped down from his navy security-guard jumper to a black T-shirt (a tight, tight black T-shirt. I noticed *that* all right), and his nose wasn't spouting blood any more. But all the same, I should have recognised him before he started talking to me, shouldn't I? Then I wouldn't have been frowning up at him so off-puttingly when he asked, ''S'it OK if I join you?'

No wonder he backed off. When I frown I look as anti-social as a pit-bull with lousy people skills. Poor Dave Griffen, retreating from my table with his hands held up in apology, must have decided I was raging with him. I'd to reassure him with my best smile when I said, 'Sure, join me. How's your sore nose?'

Smiling and speaking at once is normally something even I can manage, but unfortunately goldfish-memory girl here had forgotten I was still chewing away at my breakfast.

Dave Griffen's nice tight black T-shirt would have

had to go straight in the wash when he got home, especially after I tried to wipe off the toast I spat up over his bricklike chest with the napkin I'd used during my fry-up.

'Is this my payback, for – y'know. Over there,' Dave Griffen cocked his head towards the door of the caff. For a moment he was laughing at what I was doing, but when he said 'Over there' his smile clouded and his eyes cut from me to the street beyond then back to me. Maybe, I reckoned, armchair detective that I am, he was calculating whether it was wise for him to carry on jawing with me. Or not.

For once I was probably right.

'Listen. I honestly didn't think you were with – Didn't put you and Mr Josef toge– You're just not his –' Dave Griffen gave up on what he was trying to stammer. Sighed and shrugged, drawing an air outline of me with his open palm as if he wanted it to say what he couldn't bring himself to admit.

'You mean Stefan's a regular in that place?' I interpreted his gesture. *Along with his other babes-es. And they never look like me, do they?* I nearly added, but I decided to spare myself the stab of hearing the truth from a direct kind of fella like Dave Griffen.

'Biggest customer, by a long shot,' Dave nodded. 'He's in and out every designer shop in the city, spending like there's no –' he went on. Then stopped himself. Gave his head a shake.

'Course you'll know that,' he said, pushing back his chair. Standing. 'You're with him.'

In the space of half a sentence, Dave Griffen seemed to back right off.

'Anyway, I'm glad you're OK. Take care – sorry, I never got your name. I'm Dave.'

Dave's hand was outstretched. Thick, strong fingers jabbing mine for a parting shake.

What's your hurry? I wanted to ask, but instead I said, 'I'm Claudia,' before blurting at Dave, 'but call me Clod. Everyone calls me Clod.'

'Clod.' Dave gave my name an approving nod before he made to leave me once and for all. 'Again. Sorry about today. Truly wasn't personal, Clod,' he smiled, putting his hand to his heart. 'I mean it. You take care.' He was looking into my eyes when his smile dropped.

'Seriously. You take care,' he repeated. Then he made his way to the till.

Well, I was having none of that. First of all, I'd good news:

'Hey. Wait up. I got your job back.'

I belted across the caff before Dave Griffen could pay anything. Of course me being me, I managed to knock over two chairs and spill somebody's full teacup all over my foot in my haste.

'Run, son. She's chasing you,' a wheezy old woman piped up.

'But she's putting her money where her mouth is. I'd definitely hang on to her,' quipped another and cracked up the caff when he heard me say, 'I'll pay.'

Busy telling Dave Griffen, 'Stefan's gonna phone your boss,' I was waving a note at the caff-man. A twenty-spot, I assumed, plucked from the roll in my jeans pocket, till the caff-man shook his head, 'Isnae The Ritz, love. I canny change a fifty.'

'Both bills on me. And another tea for the one my friend spilled over there.' Dave Griffen had given the caff man a tenner before I could dig out more money from my stash.

'Better watch where you flash the cash, Clod.' His nod at the note in my hand was curt. 'In fact,' he whispered, looking me square in the eye as he cocked his head round the caff, 'I'd put it away, eh?'

There was either pity or disapproval or both in the glance he shot me as he slipped past and outside.

I was having none of that either.

'Hey, sorry. Stefan just handed me a wad of notes –'

'How the other half live. As I said, you take care.'

Out in the street, Dave Griffen started walking fast. He was passing Strut, heading for the subway. I'd to jog to keep up with him.

'You know you can go back to work now.'

'Grateful,' Dave Griffen snapped. Ungratefully. He was picking up his pace. I did the same.

'Didn't mean you to lose your job in the first place. Didn't know what was going on.'

'Your fella did. Ask him about it.'

A sleek Merc crawled along the road at the same pace I was walking. It was travelling so slowly Dave

Griffen dodged in front of it to cross the street. *To get away from me.*

'Hang on. Stefan's not my *fella*. I hardly know him. I don't have a *fella*.' I'd as much of a clue about what made me blurt these words to Dave Griffen as I'd a clue about why I told him my name was Clod. These things just came out. Loud. That's probably why the passengers in the crawling Merc rolled up their windows and swerved round me to drive off out of earshot.

It has been said that I shout like a town cryer.

'Met Stefan two days ago. Don't know *anything* about him.'

I caught up with Dave Griffen at the entrance to the subway, although I'd to queue for a ticket while he used his travel pass to beat me through the barrier. He waited on the other side of it, though.

'You *really* don't know Stephen Josef?' he asked as I came through.

'Not even his surname till you used it. Honest.'

'Well take my advice. You don't want to know him.' Dave Griffen emphasised his words by squeezing my fingers in his big hand. It was soft. So was his voice now. Friendlier. Kind. Less guarded.

'How d'you mean?' I pressed, but we became separated in the crush on the escalator down to the subway platforms and Dave Griffen was in front of me and didn't turn round to answer. Just gave me a promising smile at the bottom, 'Might see you around, Clod. When you're not involved with –'

With a wave, Dave made for the opposite platform to mine. Then he stopped. Turned back.

'Tell you what. You can buy me breakfast sometime. Got a mobile?' he asked.

part 2

a cuppa with starsky and hutch

So here was me, in a hunger or a burst situation:

Two guys in two days had my number. One of the two guys in those two days even had two mobiles. Double chance of a call! *And* not only had he punted me a juicy wad of cash for nothing, but he'd gone down on his knees *begging* me to be his babes. Mad.

Yup. A hunger or a burst situation. Or should that be burst then a hunger? Because despite Stefan's hand-on-heart promise to be in touch and Dave Griffen's slightly more lukewarm approach to seeing me again:

'Seriously, once you're shot of Mr Big, give us a call, Clod. I'd like that . . .'

Well, I didn't hear a dicky-bird. From Stefan or Dave.

Still, I couldn't exactly say I was pining. Even if I'd wanted to, there was no chance to mope – or, more constructively, to swot – in my bedroom. Far too busy

I was, in the company of two older men who seemed *desperate* to spend time with me. Not only that, whenever *they* promised to keep in touch they *always* kept their word.

I'm talking, of course, about the detective double-act: Hatch and Stark.

Starsky and Hutch.

Not to mention Marjory.

I was straight home off the subway after leaving Dave Griffen and was *literally* walking up my path, wishing it wasn't quite so long and that my stomach wasn't quite so full, and there they were. On my case. Plod-plod-plodding my still-warm footsteps in their big police-issue shoes.

'Finally –'

'– the elusive Miss Quinn. Feeling –'

'– better enough to be out and about, are you? Because –'

'– your school said you'd been phoned in –'

'– sick. Hope you're well enough –'

'– to answer –'

'– a few more –'

'– questions.'

'– questions.'

The detectives finished their introduction in perfect synchronicity. That kind of threw them, I think, because they started giving each other polite 'after you' hand signals instead of saying anything else to me.

'Oh for goodness sake. Zit all right if we come in, Claudia?'

Marjory bustled round her superiors with a cut-the-crap-before-I-knock-your-heads-together sigh. Leaving them to follow, she took my arm. Police training must involve locating the kitchen in strange houses, because she steered me straight through to ours.

Police training must also involve sniffing out the teabag jar, and where people hide their fancy biccies, because Marjory had the right cupboard in one.

(Note to self: I could do that too, so definitely consider the police as a career option. Speak to Uncle Mike asap.)

'Quick cuppa,' Marjory prescribed rather than asked me, already filling the kettle, finding a plate and fanning it with shortbread I hadn't spotted last time I searched for goodies. 'Then we'll pop you down to the station. OK?'

Marjory put her hands on my shoulders to sit me down. Looking over my head at Starksy and Hutch, she froze. It was like she was waiting for the detectives to give her the nod to proceed.

So for a few seconds, the only sound in the kitchen was the increasing roar of the kettle. Have you ever noticed how it sounds like an ominously approaching tidal wave when nobody's talking over it? Anyway, that's what I was just thinking about until Starsky-Stark or Hutch-Hatch gave a phlegmy throat clear, and Marjory hunkered down to my eye level. She plopped her big hand on my leg. Gripped my knee and shoogled it till I was looking at her.

'Right. Now we're needing you to look at some pictures, Claudia. And have another chat. Remember I said we might have to do that if the man you saw the other day –'

'I didn't see. Was hiding. Told you before,' I snapped into Marjory's words. *Too fast,* I realised. Too defensive.

So I slid my eyes away from Marjory's steady gaze.

Casually – or as casually as I could – I made myself incredibly interested in the scrap of paper Dad had left for me on the kitchen table.

Hey Cloddy. Still no sign of my licence or VISA. Now I've lost my passport too! Maybe you'll have a scout after school? Study hard. See you tonight about 7. Cheers.

I read the note three times. By then Marjory had four mugs lined up.

'Milk? Sugar?' She was asking Starsky and Hutch. They were taking seats on either side of me at the kitchen table. Closing in.

'Some of the pictures we'll show you –'

'– might jog your memory –'

'– and help us put –'

'– some dangerous men –'

'– men who kill, in fact –'

'– away.'

They relayed between noisy slurps.

'Men who kill?' I didn't even know I'd spoken

aloud but Starsky-Stark, Hutch-Hatch and Marjory were all nodding at me as if they were keeping time with an official police metronome. My voice was strangely thin and small. Little girl lost-ish.

The look on my face must have matched it because Marjory patted my hand.

'Now you can bring somebody with you,' she suggested, helping herself to a third shortbread finger. 'What about Mum?'

By the time I'd explained about Australia and the baby taking forever to be born, and Mum's open ticket meaning she could be away for weeks . . . Oh, and Neil's low sperm count (that just gabbled out) Starsky and Hutch were looking *pretty* bored. Not to mention squirmy.

'Your dad around then?' Starsky-Stark crossed his legs and asked his watch.

'See time's of the essence.' Hatch-Hutch's tone hinted that I'd be wise not to outline the current staffing shortages of Quinn's Family Eyecare to explain why Dad wasn't home.

'He's working late tonight. Won't be able to get away.' I left it at that.

'No one else close? Granny? Uncle?'

While I was shaking my head at the detectives, I scrolled my brain for anyone who could be called on at short notice to keep me company in a crisis. Pathetic this was. Embarrassing. My list of I'd-Drop-Anything-For-Clod-Quinn contacts running to an unimpressive three. *All unavailable: Georgina in Africa. Mum in Australia. Uncle Super Mike a long motorway drive away in Aberdeen.*

Marjory sussed I was floundering.

'You could always phone a friend.' She tried to throw me a line. Her voice was hopeful.

'Or a classmate?' She threw me another one. Watched me scraping the barrel.

'Never mind, I'll be with you.'

When I failed to come up with a name she leaned over and knuckled my arm with so much kindness that, instead of bursting into tears, I heard myself blurting, 'Can I bring a guy I know?'

I was meaning Stefan, of course. He counted as a 'friend', didn't he? We'd dated. Snogaroo-ed. I'd seen more of him than Dad in the last forty-eight hours.

Even better, his voice was in my head, replaying something I'm sure I hadn't just imagined he'd said: *'I'm only a phone call away when you need me, babes.'*

'Well, so long as he meets us at the station –'

'– and we move it *now* –'

'and your pal's not squeamish –'

Starky and Hutch's dialogue ping-ponged over my head as we left the house. I scrolled my mobile for Stefan's number.

Found it.

Dialled.

'Who's the lucky lad, then?' Marjory joined me in the back seat of the detective's car. Her big elbow was kidding me so hard my phone nearly flew out my hand.

'I'm still in the market myself, by the way. Ask your guy if he's got a mate who likes curling and hot curries,' she was asking but I couldn't oblige her.

I was frowning at my phone. Checking to see if I'd battery. Switching off and on again. Retrying Stefan's number. Three, four, five times.

But it didn't ring out.

'I'm sorry. The number you have dialled has not been

recognised . . .' the operator's calm voice advised me each time.

And when I texted instead, my message just bounced back to me.

20

the nicotine room

'Right, Claudia. To recap. A serious assault took place outside your dad's shop. You're inside, but you insist you saw nothing. Correct?' While DCI Starsky-Stark was asking me this question, and I was answering in my flattest you're-wasting-my time-when-I've-better-things-to-do voice: 'Yeah. Nothin',' he showed me into a room.

And bringing me down to the cop shop doesn't change anything: I saw what those hammer guys did. I'm keeping my witness statement zipped up inside me. This is what I was reminding myself as I plonked in the chair Starksy-Stark scraped back for me and checked out the inside of the first interview room I'd been in. Weird thing here is that it was *just* like one you'd see in all the telly cop programmes. It was small, drab and windowless, unless you count the grubby slatted excuse for ventilation set high in one of the nicotine-coloured walls. Despite several tatty NO SMOKING notices, the room *stank* of nicotine too. And sweat. Both smells stale and overpowering, leeching from the paintwork, the floor, the air . . .

The smell was the only detail about the room that made it different from all the ones I'd seen on telly. There was a scruffed table in the centre, like you'd have on *Prime Suspect.* Though instead of that weary old actress who won an Oscar putting on a grey wig and frowning like the Queen, I was at one side, with Marjory, Starsky and Hutch facing me. There was even a tape recorder so I half expected someone to start the interrogation intro routine you get on *Morse, The Bill, Inspector Frost* . . .

Persons present for interview: DCI Starsky-Stark and DI Hutch-Hatch, nice-but-butch Sargy-Marjory and big daft Clod Quinn.

Except this wasn't an interrogation.

'This isn't an interrogation.'

'We're just –'

'– keen to clear things up with you more –'

'– formally,' the detectives told me. While they did

so, DI Hutch-Hatch even unplugged the tape recorder and put it on the floor. This allowed more room on the table for the sheets of paper his superior was taking from a folder and, as carefully and deliberately as if he was playing patience, spread out. Before each sheet went down, the detective paused. Checked what was on it. Whatever it is, I thought to myself, must be grim, because the lines round DCI Starsky-Stark's down-turned mouth visibly deepened with each sheet he studied. Made him age before my eyes.

'Right, Claudia.'

When the DCI had five sheets laid out he folded his hands on his belly and gave me his attention. 'I just want you to look carefully at some pictures,' he said in a soft, weary voice.

shock tactics

Don't know how long I sat in that room with the detectives. An hour? A month? Two minutes? No idea. All I remembered was seeing what I saw, wishing I hadn't, wishing even more I could silence the non-stop descriptions of what I was looking at. Because the voiceover from Starsky and Hutch made it way too much. Too horrible. While the men described terrible things to me in their unflappable, grey voices I wanted to put my hands over my ears and shut out their commentary with some of my special humming. But I think I must have been holding my breath for too long because the moment I lifted my arms everything went swimmy in my head.

So as I said, I don't know how long I spent in that nicotine room. There was a blank between me sitting beside Marjory and her lugging me along a corridor to a sink, splashing cold water on my face.

'Take it you've never seen a dead person before then, Claudia?'

Only in Westerns, thrillers, slashers, horrors: Silence of the Lambs, Texas Chainsaw Massacre, Straw Dogs.

Only on the box. Where I can switch off.

Forget.

Enjoy.

I tried to answer Marjory but my words just came out as bubbly gasps. I was too traumatised by the images I'd seen on the flip-side of those sheets of paper to manage anything as ordinary as talking. I mean, I could hardly *breathe*. Or see normally, because open or closed, my eyes kept flicking through the pictures from the nicotine room like they were flash-cards I'd committed to memory:

First, in separate photographs, the detectives made me study two naked girls. They were lying on the same piece of torn lino with their arms and legs splayed into positions no female would ever choose to pose herself. Both their torsos were –

'extensively bruised –'

'– following a violent assault.'

'– Estonian, these young women, we think –'

'– on false passports, though –'

'– so we don't know their real names.'

'Anyway, as you can see, Claudia –'

'– the faces of these girls have been –'

'– well, you call what's been done excoriation –'

'Not a pretty sight –'

'– is it?'

'These girls were mules –'

'– for a crime ring we've been after –'

'– for months and –'

'– we actually had surveillance on this pair –'

'– one of our undercovers getting close to these girls –'

'– sweet girls despite their habit, apparently –'

'– anyway we're preparing to move in –'

'– find out who's pulling these lassies' strings –'

'Then they disappear.'

'And from one of the high-rises across from your dad's place at Greenwood reports come in of a bad smell –'

'And we find these young women in one of the flats –'

''Bout your age they'll be, Claudia –'

'Coroner reckons they were alive throughout their torture.'

The next photograph the detectives showed me bore no resemblance to what they described.

'Now here's the remains of a man in his fifties –'

'Pick the photo up, Claudia, to get a better look.'

'Now we know more about him than the first two bodies –'

'– because he was a security guard –'

'– and one of ours.'

'Ex-cop.'

'Retired –'

'keeping himself out of mischief with a few night shifts –'

'"And out from under my feet." That's what his wife said about –'

'– Andy. His name's Andy Muir.'

'His wife's Jess.'

'Two sons.'

'One of them about to be a dad –'

'– same as your brother is, Claudia. Coincidence, eh?'

'Anyway, Andy was a night-watchman down the freight warehouses –'

'– on the Clyde. Working for a shipping company –'

'– you'll have seen these giant containers down there –'

'– they store everything and anything –'

'– not always legal cargo.'

'Drugs, guns, people come in through these containers now and again –'

'– so one night our boys get a shout from Andy –'

'– suspicious delivery in the next yard –'

'– but the call cuts off before Andy's done talking.'

'No sign of Andy after that.'

'Jess is frantic –'

'– as you would be –'

'– if your husband disappears into the ether.'

'Then a week on some fisherman up Deeside snags –'

'– well at first he thinks it's a log –'

'– but as you'll see, Claudia –'

'– that's a partially burnt torso you're looking at.'

'Skull found intact further up the river –'

'– which meant we could identify Andy –'

'– though his arms and legs have never been found.'

'So that's Andy.'

'But this next fella here's a complete mystery-man . . .'

When Stark and Hatch moved swiftly on to the third photograph, I was almost relieved.

No more shock tactics. Just a headshot of a young guy. No blood. No bruises. No sign of violence. He looked early twenties to me: bad skin, thin blueish lips falling back from his teeth to make it hard to tell if he was smiling or sneering. I'd have judged his expression better if his eyes were open but they were closed. He looked asleep.

'Peaceful enough eh, Claudia?' The DCI tapped my thoughts as he tapped the photo. 'So far this is as much as we've got of this lad.'

'His head.'

'Found in an alley in Aberdeen.'

'No sign of the rest of him apart from –'

'– well, actually you're seeing the cleaned-up version of this poor bastard.'

'He was found with his mouth full –'

'– and a certain intimate part of his anatomy misplaced –'

'– but we'll spare you that photo –'

'– for now. It's in DCI Stark's file if you're interested.'

'Anyway Interpol –'

'– they reckon this fella's Eastern European too –'

'– can tell from his dental work –'

'– and the hallmark in his earring. And that Claudia –'

'– is us about done with what we needed to show you, apart from –'

'– this gentleman here.'

That final image on the table in the nicotine room was nothing like the others. For a start, the male subject in it was clearly alive. In fact, as he strode towards the camera, snarling something through the cigar in his teeth and giving the finger to whoever was snapping him, he looked larger than life. The closest thing to a human walrus I'd ever seen, he was, huge belly straining the white T-shirt he wore tucked into trackie bottoms mismatched with what was probably a very sharp jacket. Though it was hard to judge the quality of the threads given that the photo was so blurred. That was the second thing that made this pic different from the others the detectives had shown me. It was poor quality. Grainy. A shot of a moving target. Not a still . . . Huh. Get me: I was going to say 'still *life*'.

Still death, all the other photos were.

Anyway, in this picture I'd to peer to distinguish the smaller details, but what I made out told even a dumbo like me all I needed to know about this big man: you wouldn't mess.

Basically, from his stubby grey ponytail to his white loafers, he was a tick-the-box gangster. The bling round his neck and wrists and fingers might as well have been engraved 'BAD DUDE', and as for his enormous gold specs – well, according to my dad, that ugly brown tint was always the giveaway.

'Only clergy and crooks go for that these days. Folk with something to hide, Cloddy,' Dad would have been whispering out the side of his mouth if he'd been sat beside me instead of Marjory.

But he wasn't and Marjory wasn't whispering. She was telling me, 'Our friend here's incredibly camera-shy, but we can show you some pictures our forensics snapped when he was . . . well not exactly saying cheese, but a lot more cooperative.'

'Then, Claudia,' DCI Starsky-Stark chipped in. He was sweeping all the photographs, except the one of the walrus, into his folder. Taking more sheets from a different one, 'I'm having a cigarette and you're having a think to yourself in case there's something you remember about what you didn't see. So, eyes down –'

I recognised the hammered man from Dad's shop immediately. There were two pictures of him, taken from different angles. Both of them caught the man battered into a bloody, crumpled heap. Must have been snapped just before the paramedics attended to him.

'You know this gentleman,' the DCI swung his index finger back and forth between the walrus-gangster photo and one of the hammered man, but he kept his eyes fixed hard on me till I nodded.

'But not as well as us,' DI Hutch-Hatch took over the talking while his boss concentrated on staring me down. 'And not as well as we'd have come to know him –'

'– if someone who was even less keen on him than us hadn't taken him out.' Marjory was in on the commentary now, pulling out her notebook, puffing up her big manly chest.

'The victim of the fatal assault outside Quinn's Family Eyecare is Douglas Hall. Glasgow businessman, aged 58 –' she read formally from her notes, then she laid them aside. 'Better know as Hell Dog Hall. Complete scumbag.' Marjory narrowed her eyes, wincing as if the words she was saying were nipping her mouth. 'Drugs, guns, brothels, customs scams, illegals, false docs, fraud, dog-fighting, car-ringing. You name it, he was behind it –'

'The Glaswegian Godfather, if you like,' Starsky and Hutch couldn't seem to resist putting in their oars.

'But untouchable –'

'– or, at least he was –'

'– till someone from left field . . .'

'Look, let's get to the point about why you're here.' DCI Stark was on his feet, unlit cigarette in his mouth, box of Swan Vestas rattling in one hand, match poised for striking in the other.

'Just looking at this bastard makes me feel I need fumigating. I'll make no bones: Hell Dog was *scum*, Claudia. Involved in a world that you – a nice wee lassie – just wouldn't have a . . . Ach–'

Slumping against the doorframe of the nicotine room, DCI Stark's face when it dropped to his chest was nearly the same grey as his suit. 'Thing I'm trying to say, pet,' he went on more kindly, 'without scaring you more than you're scared already, is that while we're in here and you're saying f-all, pardon my French, somebody's out there who kills gangsters in broad daylight. And we don't know who it is yet. But it's someone with balls big enough to think he can step into Hell Dog's shoes.'

'If that makes any sense,' DI Hutch-Hatch started nodding in agreement but then he seemed puzzled. 'I mean it would be *feet* stepping into Hell Dog's shoes, wouldn't it, Boss? Not balls. You don't put your balls into shoes –'

'I've made my point, loud and clear,' DCI Starsky-Stark's glare included everyone in the nicotine room, but it lingered on me before he left.

'Better get your thinking cap back on, Claudia.'

22
beauty parade

'Him?'

'Him?'

'Them?'

'Him?'

'Them?'

'Him?'

'Them, Claudia?'

'None of them?'

'You're sure? Tell me if you need to go back to see any again.'

I was sitting next to Marjory – just the two of us now. We were alone in a different room, brighter than the last, though even smaller. It was cluttered with chairs and desks and all the clumsy space-gobbling plastic and electronic spaghetti you need to run monster computers like the one I'd been at for at least half an hour. All that time I'd been shaking my head at a monitor while Marjory showed me more photographs. File after file after file. A parade of ugly, ugly men this time, not a one I'd fancy meeting up a dark alley, or in a dream, or jumping me when I walk up my front path in the dark, let me tell you. They were either scowling out from an official police mugshot, snapped unawares by surveillance, or captured in blurry freezeframe from CCTV. None of them were saying 'cheese'.

'Any of these chaps jog your memory so far, Claudia? Remember, you give us an ID, we protect you as best we can.'

Aye right. Protect me like dead police informers on 24? Think I button up the back?

'Memory of *what*? I told you I was hiding. Behind Dad's desk. I didn't see –' Automatically I started to protest, but had to stop.

Who was I kidding?

It was obvious I was lying, my whine unconvincing and shrill, my face twitchy from the effort of trying to force it into an expression of innocence it couldn't wear. Not now. Not when I'd seen what those hammer men I wasn't telling the police about might have done to . . .

Those girls. Their faces. And that ex-cop. And the thought of that bloke's bollocks stuffed in his . . .

Marjory must have heard my sharp intake of breath because she clicked her monitor to a still of the real 1970s Starsky and Hutch. Pushed back her chair. Patted my hand.

'Take a breather. One more beauty parade, then I'll get you home. You're doing great,' she was smiling but when she looked beyond me to the mirror covering the upper part of the wall behind us, her smile drooped. She rolled her eyes.

'Is that mirror a two-way? For watching witnesses?' *Checking out if they're telling porkies or not?* I was gulping. Blushing. Mortified. Imagining some crack police psychologist with his clipboard doing his Robbie Coltrane and analysing my body language. Pointing his fountain pen at me through the two-way glass. Telling the DCI:

'She knows something, Boss. I'd lean harder. She'll talk . . .'

'You watch too much TV, Claudia.' Marjory,

chuckling at my anxiety, didn't confirm or deny my suspicions about the mirror.

'Come on,' she said. 'Just a few more upstanding citizens. Now if any of them are in the *slightest* way familiar . . .'

Click. Click. Click.

Aware of possible unseen eyes on me this time, I sat as still as I could, hands in my lap, back straight. I blinked only when a face changed on the screen. This was fine, in fact I was feeling quite smug. Smug enough to make one of my mental notes to myself:

Investigate Secret Service for possible career options. Or acting. Because whenever Marjory clicked from one mugshot to the next I could see my own face briefly reflected on the surface of her monitor, and without tooting on my own trumpet I'd say outwardly I must have looked pretty damn composed.

A cool customer. Inscrutable . . . I almost congratulated myself.

Then Marjory went and spoiled the masquerade.

'Last –'

Click.

'– group –'

Click.

She sighed.

And I jerked back in my seat like someone out the computer had socked me a right hook.

What a muppet.

The Glaswegian versions of Starsky and Hutch were panting stale coffee breath down my neck before I'd managed to resume my own involuntary respiration pattern.

'Right. You've seen this man before?'

'And that one?'

'Previous JPG, please Marj.'

'And forward –'

'– back.'

'Have another good look, Claudia.'

'You know how important it is that you help us in any way you can.'

'These are evil people we're trying to find.'

And that's basically why I'm bloody well not wanting to tell you anything. I was curling up into a tight foetal ball in my head while Marjory moused between the same two images. Both were enhanced stills from a piece of video footage. This meant that in close-up, the two men leaving a car looked blurry and distorted enough to be drawn on soggy blotting paper rather than made of flesh and bone and hair. Like the badge on their Mercedes, only the men's most distinguishing characteristics jumped out at me.

But it was these I'd recognised. Instantly.

The monobrow of the darker, thickset man. The monobrow beneath which his hard, black eyes had scanned Dad's shop. The memory made me wince.

So did the jutty angles of his fairer companion. The jumpy headcase with boxer's footwork. Seeing him again made me catch my breath with a squeak. Hold it. And the hint of rings on every finger curving the pixels of the hands resting on the car doors . . .

That's what made me scrape back my chair. Remembering. Those fingers. Twice I'd seen them. The first time they'd sliced through Hell Dog Hall's hair. The second time, similar ringed fingers were attached to whoever drove . . .

. . . whoever drove *Stefan,* my sweet-talking guy,

into his garage. *Although Stefan's driver can't have had anything to do with this scowler on Marjory's computer. Loads of blokes wear chavvy rings,* I was telling myself as I shrank from the stares of the cruel men I'd seen outside Dad's shop. *Stefan's driver's rings just triggered a flashback of the hammer scene . . .*

'So. Finally we've jogged that memory of yours, Claudia.' Starsky-Stark gave my shoulder a grateful squeeze. But his voice was the gravest I'd heard it and when I opened my mouth to stutter the usual denial – 'B-b-ut I didn't say . . .' – he'd his palm flatted a millimetre from my face.

'As an old Kojak song goes: "If a face could paint a thousand words –"' His finger drew a circle in the air round my head and shoulders. 'You clearly recognise these men.'

'I . . . uh . . .'

'A nod'll do. Don't bother with another lie. And by the way, I'm warning you formally: your wise monkey act comes under wasting police time. That's chargeable.'

'So you've seen these men before, Claudia?' While

her DI struck the monitor with sharp, impatient raps of his pen, Marjory bumped my arm with her elbow. Ouch! For some reason her softly-softly tactics brought tears to my eyes.

'We're done here. Promise.' Marjory was nodding at me as she spoke, half-smiling, like she was my friend, like we were in cahoots against the detectives. I felt my head nodding in symmetry with hers before I could bring down a shutter on her kindness. I was tired. My brain hurt.

'That's a yes. Take the lassie home.' DCI Starsky-Stark spat a fleck of tobacco from the unlit cigarette in his mouth.

'Just as we thought,' he sighed. 'This silent witness here saw Humpty and Dumpty all along. Bugger it.' His head-jerk was sheer impatience as he held the door open for his DI to follow him from the room.

'Now we need to find who's yanking their chains –'

'Chase down the organ grinder –'

I could hear the detectives muttering curses to each other as they swept from the room like they were too busy to waste another second in my company.

'C'mon lady. You've done good. Let's get outa here and get ourselves something to eat.' When she clicked her tongue at me, chuckling at her crappy American accent, I suddenly realised how much kind and well-meaning Sargy-Margy was reminding me of another cop: *That pregnant one. Another Marge. From Georgina's favourite film.* Fargo. *About a horrible murder . . .*

The coincidence made me gasp. Made me wish, more than anything, that *my* Marge and I could just be film characters too. Could leave the set. Walk away . . .

off down under

'Cloddy, did you even *bother* yourself to look for my passport? I've turned the house upside down. Your mum swears it's in her dressing-table drawer. But it's not. I've wasted an afternoon queuing in the passport office for a temporary. Then I'd to get a new credit card sorted and I nearly didn't. Been fighting with the bank. My VISA's been skimmed or scammed or cloned, so they tell me. Couldn't buy my flight with it. It's maxed out –'

Apart from the fact he was yakking non-stop, I knew my dad was hyper as soon as he opened the front door. He was topless for starters, although he *was* wearing a towel round his waist and a pair of Mum's reading glasses. Retro, rhinestone-studded batgirl ones complete with a sparkly spec-chain which was buried in the tangle of his furry chest rug.

Combined with the state of Dad's hair, which was

completely standing on end and bushed out round his ears, the whole effect made him look like a camp hobbit with a taste for bling.

'I'm off Down Under. In an hour.'

Oblivious to the burly policewoman who'd escorted me home, Dad was flapping an airline ticket so close to Sargy-Margy's face that she had to reel back.

'Neil's had the baby but he's awful weak,' Dad kept on flapping. 'Your mother wants me over in case things . . .'

Sicko that I am, you've no idea how close I was to cracking out one of my tasteless funnies: *No wonder Neil's weak if he's just performed the miracle of birth* I almost blurted, but I managed to bite my tongue. Glad I did, because I realised my dad had actually reached meltdown, and what he was saying was no joke.

'Baby's had an operation already. Wee scrap, your mother says. Fighting for his life. Called him Sean . . . Isn't that just? . . . Oh I don't know what to take with me. Your mother always packs my . . . and the whole day's been utter hassle . . . I've had to arrange locums for the shop and now I can't find . . .'

Suddenly, the adrenalin that was keeping my dad together seemed to evaporate. He literally slid down the hall wall till his bum met the carpet.

Burying his face in his knees, his fingers of one hand shredded his hair. The other gestured pathetically at his open suitcase. So far he'd packed two odd socks.

I had to hand it to Marjory. People always accuse cops of being a waste of time, don't they? Never about when you need them. But I doubt Dad would've have packed much more than those sad socks, let alone made his flight if it hadn't been for a certain police presence in our house that night. Think I'd have known where Dad hid his underpants? His blood pressure tablets? I was standing over him gawping and Marjory was already in Public Assistance Mode, crouched down next to him, plucking the plane ticket from his hand, checking the time of his flight.

'Hello, Mr Quinn. Remember me? Marjory? From your shop the other day. Now don't be alarmed about seeing Claudia with a police officer. She's not done anything wrong. She's been trying to help us identify the men who were involved in the attack there. I need to talk to you about that but first we'll get you sorted for your plane. You've less than an hour before check-in.'

Marjory spoke to my dad using one of the slightly patronising shouty voices the chirpy emergency services people on reality TV shows save for vagrants or old dears who've broken a hip. While she spoke she reassured him with big capable pats to his knee.

'Come on now, sir.'

The capable pats became firmer until my dad lifted his head and frowned at Marjory like she was an annoying stranger.

'Will Claudia be going with you? To Australia? Should she be packing?' Marjory raised her voice to hold my dad's attention. 'Or is she staying here by herself?'

My dad shook his head.

'Your mum doesn't want you missing school,' he answered me, not Marjory. 'Says you'll be fine on your own for a few days and there's no point you moping about a hospital saying you're bored and hungry and annoying everybody with your humming. But if you pass your resits Mum says we'll send you to Australia for Christmas to get to know your . . . That's if the wee soul . . . Did I tell you how sick he is? Sean they've called him . . .' My dad's head, after a blurt of almost sensible talking, was threatening to bury itself in his knees again. Marjory grabbed his hand. Hauled him to his feet.

'You need to focus now, Mr Quinn. Claudia's going to help with your toilet stuff and I'll find you some clothes.'

Taking Dad's arm, Marjory clomped him upstairs. In the time it took me to collect Dad's shaving kit and toothbrush from the bathroom, Marjory had sorted his suitcase.

'Undies, shirts, shorts and trousers. See? And I've left that space for toiletries and gadgets. All right, Mr Quinn? I think you should put this top on for travelling. And I'd definitely wear underpants. Claudia can find you some. Here she is.'

Dad, towel all bagged round his lower half like a helpless toddler in a giant nappy, was sagged on Mum's dressing-table stool. When I held out a jumper for him to wear he made no effort to take it and dress himself.

I'd to pull it over his head, force his arms into the sleeves. While I was struggling with that, Marjory was in Dad's wardrobe clanging coathangers together. One by one she pulled out all Dad's jackets and held them against herself in front of Mum's long mirror.

'Why's a policewoman going through my clothes?' my dad asked when I lifted Mum's batgirl glasses from his face and he was able to see in the distance again. He scrunched his face at the sight of Marjory smoothing his sports jacket over her bust, admiring herself from different angles. 'Oh, take this Harris tweed, Mr Quinn. Wear it to the airport and you could get an upgrade.'

Marjory peeled Dad's jacket from her police tunic and came round behind him, holding it out for Dad to slip on.

'Now we're all packed I'll call the airline. Explain your circumstances. And don't worry about Claudia while you're out the country; we'll keep an eye out for her – arm in here for me, sir,' she coaxed Dad. He put one arm in his sleeve. Then he stopped, letting his jacket slip to the floor.

'Why are you in my bedroom?'

Dressed in sensible clothes, Dad was suddenly more collected. 'Are you to do with losing my passport and the VISA? I didn't contact you lot yet. Too busy.' He turned from Marjory to Mum's dressing table. Yanked Mum's jewellery drawer out so roughly that half her earrings and bangles and bracelets bounced out the sides of it, rolling and tumbling to the carpet. 'I told them at the bank and the passport office: how can a passport and a VISA be stolen from my house when there's been no break-in –'

'Sure about that, sir?'

'I'd know if an intruder had been through my own drawers, wouldn't you?' Dad snapped at Marjory from inside the top I'd dressed him in. He was pulling it off. 'Your mother'll have shoved them in with all the clutter she takes abroad and never uses.'

Dad buttoned himself up all wrong into a denim shirt, snapping at me now. 'I told Grace to look through her bags when I spoke to her earlier because I know your mother and I'll bet you, Cloddy –' Dad vented his frustration by booting his sports jacket across the bedroom, 'I'll open her handbag in Melbourne and I'll find the lot: VISA, passport, licence, kitchen sink . . .'

When Dad ran out of steam again and slumped, head in hands, on to his bed, he reminded me of the creepy kinetic automata that freaked my dreams for weeks after he took me to see them in some museum donkeys ago. One minute the puppets were manic, arms and legs flicking and kicking and jerking obscenely and dancing to crazy speeded-up music. Then suddenly they were inert, inanimate, faces frozen and blank. Staring into space, just like Dad. Till Sarge-Marge came to the rescue again.

'Make a quick cuppa for your dad. Plenty sugar.' She thumbed me from the room. 'Then I'll run you to the airport, sir. And give me details about the items you're missing and I'll look into it. You've lost passport, VISA and driving licence. Nothing else?'

All the way down to the kitchen I listened to Marjory booming at my dad.

'And there's been no forced entry, sir? No chance

you left a window open for a sneak thief?'

'Window's painted shut,' Dad rumbled back.

'No tradesman about the place you don't know well? Strangers?'

'Strangers? Don't be ridiculous.'

I was at the bottom of the stairs when my dad spluttered his response this time. *Zzzzip* his suitcase dismissed the very idea.

'Do you have strange men hanging about *your* bedroom?' he asked Marjory but before she'd a chance to answer he went on, 'Look, I've sorted out the passport for Australia, and I won't be driving while I'm there and the bank won't bill me for the VISA fraud –'

Dad's suitcase was on the first leg of its journey to Australia. He was hauling it down our stairs. Mum would have *slaughtered* him if she'd caught him scuffing the woodwork like that, but I don't think Dad noticed the scratches he was leaving. 'D'you know in a day and a half someone was spending *thousands* on my card. Ten grand nearly. Hundreds in some clothes shop here in Glasgow.'

BUMP went the case.

'Then even more on jewellery in London –'

BUMP

'– and a night in some flash hotel –'

BUMP

'– plus a load of flights to Heathrow from Estonia or somewhere like that that probably doesn't have a runway.'

BUMP

Dad's voice was growing louder. Not just because he was nearly at the bottom of the stairs. The info he was giving Marjory was cranking up his blood pressure.

'D' you know what? Before they cancelled my card some jumped-up call centre jobsworth asked me if I was sure I hadn't booked all these flights myself and forgotten about them. Or given someone my details. Like I'd do something like that –'

'Well, sir, that would just be procedure to rule you out for the fraud. Ten grand's a big spending spree for a thief to get away with. You've been unlucky. Well VISA has now.' Marjory and my dad were approaching the kitchen together. 'When a customer burns plastic up to the limit like that they're usually asked to give passwords and dates of birth before all the sales go through. It's strange so many big transactions were allowed without the card being blocked and VISA getting in touch with you. Because your spending pattern had changed. Anyway,' Marjory was right outside the kitchen door, 'at least you've cancelled the credit card now, sir.'

Despite the spatter of water gushing into the kettle I was filling, I heard every word Marjory said. And it drained the blood from my arms so instantly that I dropped the kettle into the sink. I had to lean my elbows on the edge of it to stop my knees buckling.

'At least you've cancelled the credit card now, sir.' Marjory's words seemed to ricochet off all the kitchen surfaces.

Water sprayed *everywhere*. Over my jeans and my T-shirt, across the kitchen counters, into what was left of the packet of shortbread.

'Flood,' Marjory bellowed in my ear when she caught me at the sink; cold tap full blast, kettle overflowing underneath it. Me frozen. Gulping. *Dad shouldn't have needed to cancel the card.*

'Chop, chop, Sleeping Beauty.'

Shooing me aside, Marjory turned off taps and swabbed and sluiced the worktops down. Plugged in the kettle. I didn't move out of her way, though. Couldn't.

I was zombified.

Staring at the kitchen phone.

I was seeing the only recent stranger to our house speaking into it.

A stranger my dad knew nothing about.

And I was seeing this stranger while he drew a loveheart round my dad's password: CLODDY.

Asked for our secret numbers.

Which I gave him.

Couldn't hear what the stranger was saying because my head was still clanging with Marjory's last comment to my dad.

Stefan told me everything was sorted. ***He*** *cancelled the card, or so he said.*

After *I found him:*

A strange man in Mum and Dad's bedroom.

But he wouldn't have.

The inside of my mouth was a kettle boiled dry. I tried to gulp saliva into it.

He *couldn't* have.

Not Stefan.

Not my sweet-talking guy.

all by myself . . .

Petrified about what I might splurt about Stefan before I'd had time to figure if *any* of it was possible –

Why would he nick anything?

I barely opened my mouth in the half hour before Dad left for the airport. Hummed tunelessly instead. Reading me all wrong, Dad assumed my zipped lips were due to pre-Empty butterflies.

'Don't worry,' he reassured me out on the pavement as Marjory was shotputting Dad's suitcase into her boot. 'The neighbours know you're home alone, Cloddy.'

This comment, fluffy as Milky Way on the outside, was also Dad double-speak for 'no drunken shindigs, all right?'

'Oh, and I've spoken to your Uncle Mike. He knows you're alone, too. Turns out he's coming down to Glasgow in the next day or so. Not exactly sure when, but he'll bunk at ours. Save the taxpayer a few quid on his usual hotel bill. This is my brother. Same line of business as yourself,' Dad explained to Marjory while she was opening her passenger door for him. 'Big chief honcho up north. Heard of him? Mike Quinn?' That news stopped Marjory in her tracks. For the first time since we'd met she sounded almost feminine.

'Not Super Mike? Peterhead? Oh, he's a *star.* And it's *us* he's coming to liaise with,' her deep voice did its best to giggle. 'We're working with him. National task force. The boss has just briefed him about that attack. Outside your shop. Could be part of the same case. Those men. With the hammer. Those ones you've identified, Claudia –'

Marjory was positively skittish now, words puffing out in breathless gasps each time she stabbed her chest with both thumbs to illustrate how the Strathclyde polis were working with Uncle Super Mike's division in the North-East.

'Same investigation. *Massive.* Europe wide. Investigating this crime ring. Drugs and vice. Small, small world, sir, as they say. On that Disney ride: *It's a small world after all, it's a small world after all.* You know the one I mean?'

Rather Dad than me, stuck with Marjory singing bass all the way to the airport.

'I can't believe this. What a coincidence. Super Mike. You'll feel safer in this big house when *he's* around, Claudia. I might pop round myself, let him keep an eye on *me*.' While Marge was living out some secret fantasy with *my* uncle, Dad beckoned me to the passenger window. He took my hand. Pressed a far smaller quantity of notes into my palm than I'd been given by a certain person I daren't mention to Dad in case he had a stroke. Dad squeezed my fingers shut over the money. Kissed my knuckles.

'Say a prayer for wee Sean. Work hard, be good and look after yourself, Claudia,' he managed to whisper just before Marjory leaned across him. Stubbing a big thumbs-up at me she winked, 'Remember, I'll be on the end of the phone if you need me. Soon as we round up those men you recognised, we'll bring you down for an ID parade. See you then.' *Can't wait.* I shivered while I watched the police car drive Dad off. *Claudia. You never call me that, Dad,* I thought.

Am I the only person who's suddenly felt their home didn't feel like home any more when the other people who lived in it went away? I don't mean to the supermarket or work or the pub, but on a proper journey: Plane. Train. It was so weird. Once I waved Dad out of sight and stepped back through our front door, it was like Loneliness clanked in to keep me company.

Don't go. Come back, the bricks and mortar seemed to pine.

I didn't know what to do with myself. On the kitchen table a wisp of steam was still rising from Dad's mug of hardly-sipped tea. I wrapped my hands round it. Tried to make myself stop thinking how our house had never felt colder. Less safe. The distance to the nearest neighbour so far. The pathway to the street so long. So overgrown.

I realised, of course, that I was missing a trick. Here was me with my first ever proper Empty: *party time,* as just about *anyone* I knew would be whooping if they were standing here, in my kitchen, in my big Clod clogs. They'd have made calls already: *Spread the word, gonna?* Posted an invite on the Web. *Come on over.* There'd be just about time to compile a dance playlist before the doorbell was red hot, house heaving to the rafters, slopped bev stickying everyones' party shoes to Mum's good floors. Even though it was a school night, less than a week before exam-time, even though none of the folk who'd show at my party were mates:

Whose Empty is this? Claudia Quinn? Who? Oh her? The big galoot who failed everything last year and who's a total random since her mate left?

But they'd still come to my party. It would last all week if I wanted it to. Night and day.

But, even though I knew a hardcore Empty might have made me more popular, or at least less invisible to my yearmates, I wasn't tempted. Wasn't in the mood. Even though I hated the silence around me, and a party would have drowned the silence. Which wasn't silent at all anyway. Silence never is.

Haaaaaaahhhh it swirled around me, breathing down my neck, into my ear, forcing me to beat a retreat to the only place in the house I knew wouldn't feel abandoned. My room. But even walking upstairs was a different experience to how it felt when Mum and Dad were around. *Eeeek-eeeeee* every tread creaked beneath my feet like it was sadistically out to spook me. And when I wandered into Mum and Dad's bedroom to turn out a lamp the door clicked shut on me, making me spin round, heart vaulting from my mouth. I couldn't remember the door ever doing that before. Nearly shat a brick.

Then the phone calls started.

Honestly. Just the bell shrilling through our big empty house the first time was bad enough.

I squealed higher than poor Squeally, the ex-pet mouse I fed to death used to squeal whenever I trod on her tail.

But when I picked the phone up and no one answered . . .

I mean, of all the nights for some psychic eejit to plough the phone book, select **Quinn, Sean** at random, then churn up my guts with silent phone calls: *I'm sensing a jumpy girl in a big house All By Herself. Let's get dialling.*

Actually only the first few calls were silent.

'Hello?'

Nothing.

'Hello? Hel-*low*?' That happened twice, each call only lasting a few seconds before whoever was on the other end clicked the phone down.

That was the main thing *about* those two calls that was disconcerting.

Proved someone was there.

So the third time I was a bit more pro-active.

'He-**llo** again.'

Nothing.

'Look. If this is a wind-up, gonna stop.' This time *I* put the phone down. Bang! Dialled 1471.

We do not have the caller's number said the calm lady from the phone company. Surprise, surprise. So when the fourth call came, I hardly gave it the chance to ring.

'Get stuffed ya muppet!' I snarled into the receiver. Just take a flying fu–'

'Claudia!'

'Mum?'

Ooops. She sounded a bit shocked, my poor

Mumsie, what with being such a lady. And that was before I swore.

'Did I disturb you? Are you studying, darling?' her questions travelled one way across the world while mine, 'Have you been trying to get through, Mum?' crossed them in the opposite direction. This was one of those long-distance calls with a delay that drives you spare. Means a proper conversation is impossible.

'Is your dad gone? The baby's pulling through. Isn't that lovely? And he's so beautiful. We're laughing; he's got your big feet.' It felt like Mum took five light years to tell me while I interrupted her with the very questions and answers she was looking for: 'Dad's on his way. How's the baby? Oh, that's great! What's Sean look like?'

Then we'd rung off. 'I'll phone back from a landline when Dad comes, darling. This mobile's dreadful. Look after yourself.' I wished I hadn't sounded so narked by the pauses on the line.

'Fine, Mum.'

'Bye, Mum.'

'You're breaking up, Mum.' I'd snapped to bring the call to an end. Now, having had Mum closer than she'd been for days, then letting her go, I felt lonelier than ever.

25

dangerous mint

Even though less than twelve hours from now I knew I'd be sweating through a timed essay: Mussolini's Dictatorship – Good or Bad? under exam conditions, and had done No Revision Whatsoever, I wasn't exactly in the mood to get stuck into swotting. (Was I ever?)

So I cracked open a can of Dad's Guiness – *No lady's beverage,* as Mum calls it, which is one of the reasons I like it so much. Another is the taste. Bitter thickness; nothing like it. Worth every sip of its 600 calories a pint. While the creamy head settled in the glass, I booted up my computer, lowered one of those amazingly sticky Buttermint boulders into place behind my bottom front teeth. Then I started my weekly email to Georgina.

Guess what? I'm All By Myself.

Like always, I dictated my news aloud so I could kid myself me and G were gabbing face to face. I even hummed *All By Myself* à la Celine, nasal and swoopy and – thanks to the slow dissolve of the buttermint, lispy and slavery – imagining Georgina duetting with me, her voice much trillier and school choiry. We'd only ever get through a few bars of silly singing like that before hysterics took over.

– and I'm an aunty now,

I went on, telling her about baby Sean and him being poorly and my dad jetting off to see his grandson.

Just in case things don't . . .

I deleted that last sentence as soon I heard myself saying it. Swallowed my words in a minty gulp. Call me superstitious but I didn't feel it was a smart idea to tempt fate by putting the worst-case scenario in writing.

Anyway, Mum says she'll send me out to meet *my*

nephew later this year if I knuckle down,

I dictated instead.

But oh GAWD!!!! I just can't. There's more chance I'll marry Elvis than pass anything. I've done zero work. So I'll be dead and buried by the time you come home! You've seen and heard my mumsie on the warpath so you know what she'll do to me if I fail two years running. Anyway. Hey,

I wanted to change the subject,

see if I do live to go to OZ you so HAVE to come with me. Aunty Clod and Aunty George can lullaby baby Sean with our beeyoootieefool singing. Yeah?

Right. OK that's enough about the baby. Time to tell you what's happened to ME this week. You'd better be sitting down in your mudhut, G. Coz you won't *believe* this . . .

There were *six* more silent calls while I type-talked Georgina through the Three Most Amazing Days in the

Life of Clod since the hammer attack. It was my longest ever email – a four butterminter by the time I'd filled Georgina in on what the thugs at Dad's window looked like.

How I'd been interrogated by Starsky and Hutch.

Then picked up at a sweetie counter by the tastiest guy.

Who wined and dined and even kissed me.

Took me to his flash flat.

Didn't try it on, alas and alack.

But took me shopping.

When I met another guy . . .

. . . well fit too, by the way. Dave he's called and he threw himself on top of me . . . then gave me his phone number!!!! How mad is that?

I even told Georgina how I was receiving silent phone calls as I typed my email. Then I explained how I was tackling the sixth one.

I've just kept it ringing all this time I've been telling you about Stefan's mobile going dead on me. Hey, by the way, what d'you make of that? Hope he's not a piece of crap, G! coz he's a major babe, Anyway, I've cued 'Shut Up Shut Up' on I-tunes and I've turned the volume full and I'm picking up the phone now and –

Well I just kept starting the song over and over: 'Shut up. Just shut up. Shut up . . .' About twenty times. Then, not even putting the receiver to my ear I plucked the buttermint out my mouth to bawl, **'I'm calling the police now. My uncle's a Chief Superintendent,'** into the mouthpiece. Then left the phone off the hook while I finished off my email.

Result.

I reported to Georgina.

Who's the joker, though? Bet it's that no-tits Linda. She hates me because she tripped over my feet in front of Tam Moore last week and her skirt split up the back and you could see her pants and Tam totally pissed himself laughing at her and he gave me a round of applause. Anyway, hope it *is* Linda. Not some stalker out there. Or a perv. Spying from the garden, ready to sneak in and saw me up and I'll lie here rotting till Dad comes back and opens the front door and the strench of rotting flesh makes him gag and he covers his mouth and staggers upstairs and finds me writhing full of maggots and swarming with bluebottles like the Glutton corpse in *Seven.* Oh G!! That's enough of the Scary Movie stuff. Just remember, OK? See if something horrible *does* happen, better save this email so you can show it to Starsky and Hutch as evidence. Ha! Ha!

Anyway, better go. Luv to Adrian. And lotsaluv to you. E-back what you think of MY new MAN!!!! Still can't believe a hottie so sweet wants to date me!!! Something to tell my grandchildren if I ever land a bloke who wants to bada bing me. Anyway, let's not go there: Stefan hasn't yet.

Hope he's not gay!!! Coz he's something else! If he's still MY BOYFRIEND when you come back you've gotta meet him . . .

Two things dawned on me after I clicked *SEND* and the little wingy icon fluttered my thoughts and words and deeds away to Georgina. First of all I wished I hadn't raised any of the stalker and the corpse-with-maggots stuff. Not tonight. Coz not all of it flew off with the email. Some of it flew up my nose and into my mind. Now it was worrying me. Making me hear noises that weren't there: shuffles downstairs, creaks next door, footsteps in the loft. Arggg! Should have deleted all that freak-yourself-out stuff like I deleted the worst-case scenario sentence about baby Sean.

After all – and this was the second thing that dawned on me – I HADN'T included anything in my email to Georgina about Dad's cloned VISA and his missing passport problems and how all that only happened *after* my new boyfriend wandered into a room he should NOT have been in. Accidentally on purpose I'd left out that little snippet of dodgy information about Stefan.

Actually, to be honest, I'd also accidentally-on-purpose skipped telling Georgina a few other snippets about Stefan: his evil, *so* not class snake tattoo, his attempts to force wine down me in his flat when I didn't want any. Then him rough-snogging me in his garage, not to mention turning all Don Corleone on Dave Griffen . . .

I didn't let Georgina into any of this because she's totally crammed with brains (why we're best pals I don't know since my head's as empty as a tube of Pringles five minutes after I pop and don't stop). Georgina – who plans to be a psychiatrist – is always trying to figure what she thinks people *really* mean when they say something, and has this theory that the language we use when we talk to each other is only the tip of the iceberg.

What we don't *say is more important that what we do,* G believes. *That's what I like to winkle out.*

Well, I didn't want Georgina winkling anything out from what I did or didn't say in my email. Not about Stefan. No thanks. Not yet. Not when my brain was already trying to build a worst-case scenario about who I didn't want him to be.

He can't be a thief. Or a bad guy. He's too smart. Bit of

class. And NOTHING like the gangsters and thugs down at the station today in those photos. I swallowed the idea with the dregs of my Guinness. *Just* missed sluicing the brand new mint I'd popped down with it. Lucky, I bit down hard and just about clamped the sweet between my back teeth before it slid down and choked me. Recovered, I went back to thinking about Stefan: *When he phones again,* I promised myself, *I'll ask him straight if he nicked Dad's card. In fact* – I checked my mobile was switched on.

Found Stefan's number. Rang him.

But the connection was still dead.

So in case I'd missed a text from him, my thumb idled through my Inbox:

No new messages.

No new voicemail.

'Where *are* you?' I'd to sidewaggle my jaw to speak. A boulder of buttermint was cementing my top molars to the bottom ones on one side. And it wouldn't budge.

'Oh well.' My sigh over not hearing Stefan's voice wanted to turn into a yawn now. A big one, flaring my nostrils already, pushing down softly but firmly at the muscles of my mouth. You never think of yawns being macho, but they must be. Because – think about it – even when you try to stifle them you can't. Not completely. When tsunami-sized ones, like the one swelling up inside my mouth want out, they just force themselves.

Even through teeth glued shut with sugar they force themselves, ripping molars from their moorings.

'Ouch!' By the time my yawn swept though me, half a tooth and a big silver filling were impaled in the slippery buttermint which plopped into my hand. Inhaled air converted into electric-shock tinfoil agony when it hit the newly excavated *cavern* at the back of my mouth – Great! – and when my tongue probed about I shot so high in the air I headered my lampshade and the bulb went out. Every nerve, not just the one in my exposed tooth, jarred and jangled. That explains why my thumb, still curled round my mobile, suddenly jerked. Hit a number. Dialled. In the seconds before my dental crisis I'd been scrolling through my pitifully small address book: Dad, Mum,

Georgina, couple of girls I pestered for homework help. Stefan, of course –

Now my thumb had called Dave Griffen.

'Dave Griffen?'

Through a mush of head-pain I recalled the security guard putting his number in my phone. Telling me to call him when I wasn't Stefan's girl any more.

'Oh God,' I groaned. Whether I was still or had even ever *been* Stefan's girl this was no longer an urgent priority. Controlling the raging agony in my jaw was more important. Forgetting about axe-murderers lying in wait for me beyond my room, not even bothering with lights, I moaned my way into the bathroom praying I'd find painkillers.

'Or clove oil.'

I'd forgotten I was still holding my mobile. Forgotten I'd dialled Dave Griffen at random.

So when my accidental call was answered I was very confused.

'Who this?'

Despite my phone being miles from my ear I clearly heard a guttural male voice against a background of yelling. And despite the distraction of my toothache I knew he wasn't Dave Griffen. Dave Griffen wasn't foreign. And there was no reason why his voice could ever have reminded me of the skinny nutter who'd pranced and danced outside Dad's shop, kicking Hell Dog Hall to death.

'Dave?'

'Who speak? Who want Dave?' The second time the man shouted there was no background rammy. Just a listening silence.

'Claudia. Cloddy, I mean,' I answered automatically although something was telling me I shouldn't be saying anything back to the voice on the other end of the phone.

But it was too late.

'Claudia.' The angry, shouting, foreign voice repeated my name.

Deliberately. This time the silence behind him was a thinking one. It ticked for a few seconds. Ended with a noise that I just knew was someone being slapped. Hard.

'Ayahhh!' The cry from this new male voice

suggested pain on a par with my toothache. 'Watch out, Cl–' it went on before the angry shouting man shouted it down. Yelled, 'Wrong number!' at me.

Cut the call.

open wide time

Get real. You don't know the slapped guy was saying 'Claudia'! Loads of names begin like yours: Clare, Clementine, Chloe, Cleopatra, Claudette, Clareeeeeessssss . . .

And you don't know he'd been slapped either.

Could've been Dave Griffen's mates. Messing.

You barely know the guy, after all.

And you ***definitely*** *don't know it was his proper number you rang.*

He could've stuck a wrong digit into your moby.

Slip of the finger. It happens.

So bet you ***did*** *ring a wrong number. Like the angry man said.*

And there are loads of reasons why it's dead every time you ring back . . .

'So please, please, *please* go to sleep now.'

Seven hours of non-stop tossing and turning after I

went to bed, I was still pleading with myself. Still trying to shut down my thoughts. Although, since I wanted to beat the rush for an emergency dental appointment, it was time to get up.

Like an annoying kid brother you don't want anywhere near your bedroom, daylight was creeping under the curtains already, and I hadn't slept a wink. Despite tossing back a neat whisky (*Note to self: Dad's wrong: A medicinal wonder my arse! Does it hell knock you out*) and stuffing a wodge of clove-soaked cotton wool in my poor tooth, it had throbbed all night. So had my brain. It niggled and needled me over that accidental call I might have made to Dave Griffen's mobile.

If it even was his mobile in the first place . . .

'Oh, don't start. Forget it.' I hauled myself out of bed, queasy from the bitter sweetness of clove-tinged whisky furring my tongue. The inside of my skull felt like moosh.

'The crappest night,' I spluttered under the shower, wincing when water scalded the exposed nerves in my tooth. Great, the pain reminded me: a crappier few hours ahoy.

But no Mussolini essay today. There was something. Another school skive! I only realised this when my dentist's receptionist told me to expect a fair wait till I could be seen. Pain or no pain, that cheered me up instantly! Settling into the comfiest-looking chair in the waiting room, I almost chuckled. This was despite regular reminders of impending torture from the duelling drills whirring up and down the pain octave in surgeries beyond the walls. I searched through my dentist's out-of-date pile for the mag with least writing and the most pictures. To keep calm I made a mental list of the treats I'd lavish on myself if I behaved during Open Wide Time and didn't, as on my last visit, bite Mr *This Won't Hurt* while he was numbing my mouth. Drilled and filled, I'd have an afternoon of convalescence; little nap perhaps. A DVD. A Chinese. *And who knows,* I promised myself, *there might be a call from –*

'Stefan?!?'

OH MY GOD! When I saw what I saw in the Scottish

celeb mag I was flicking . . . Or rather when I saw *who* I saw, I yelped so loud the receptionist burst into the waiting room. 'All right, Claudia?'

'Just my tooth. Aw!' I lied, although the photograph I was staring at was worse for my nerves than root canal treatment without pain relief.

There was my sweet-talking guy. Stefan . . . Only not exactly as I knew him. He was posing in a line-up of Premier Division footballers and their WAGS and STV newsreaders and weathergirls in their gladrags. He was all Jay Gatsby spivved in a white tuxedo. Slicked back hair. He'd his left arm slung over a blonde, his right circling the waist of a wasted-looking redhead. Gorgeous she was though: small-boned, creamy skinned. About half the width and height of me. Stefan had her pulled very close to him. Hip to hip they were, his eyes laughing into hers.

Or *was* it Stefan in the picture?

Was it?

I stared and stared, doing all I could to convince myself: Nah. But the harder I stared, the trickier it became to deny it was anyone else.

Even though the information on the photograph's caption was wrong:

Glasgow promoter Mr Joe and mystery companions celebrate the opening of Shocking! Scotland's exclusive members' only nightclub.

He's not a promoter. And he's not called Joe . . .

'That can't be Stefan,' I tried to reassure myself yet again. But unless Stefan had an identical twin, who was I kidding? There was *my* Stefan's smile. His dimples. I could even see the head of that snake tattooed on his wrist. It peeked beneath the cuff of the hand draping the breast of the blonde.

A couple of hours later, when my dentist whipped off his safety glasses, bared his perfect teeth at me and said, 'I'd to dig right down to New Zealand for the root of *that* one,' it didn't twig that I'd lost a tooth. Not until he rattled a plastic jar at me. 'Give that whopper to your boyfriend to wear round his neck as a love-token,' he chuckled at me. When I didn't laugh back he frowned.

'Sore? Or still numb?'

I shook my head. *Both. Very,* was the truth. Though the way I was feeling had nothing to do with the dentist. NO. My *real* pain started when I set eyes on that photograph. Now it was twisting my guts, leaving me way more distressed than last night's toothache.

Thought you weren't really one for the ladies, so what's the deal here? And you told me you'd no girlfriend. So who are your mystery companions? And I thought you were a student. Helping run your dad's business. How come you're posing for the High Life pages? Using a different name?

These puzzles tormented me all the way home. I'd walk a few steps. Stop.

Unfold the page I'd ripped from the magazine.

Who are you? I kept asking the smoothie guy in the tuxedo, wanting him to look me in the eye and give me some answers. *'And who's* ***she****?'*

A fix of chocolate might console me, I decided, but d'you know what?

Standing in the nearest newsagent's, swithering between a Mars Bar or a Topic, I realised that even the pleasure of eating chocolate would never be the same again. Thanks very much, Stefan. As for Minstrels, I'd never eat another. Couldn't even bear to look at the shiny brown packets of my favourite sweeties of all time. Alas and alack, the very sight of them time-travelled me to a different newsagent's where a guy in a suede jacket appeared beside me out of nowhere and spoke in my ear, and his fingers brushed mine and we talked and he asked me out and everything seemed to be just . . .

Too good to be true. I grabbed a box of Maltesers. Handed the newsagent a fiver. *You hardly knew the guy anyway,* I told myself. *He was just there. Never did find out why.*

Waiting for my change it dawned on me that I'd never even winkled out Stefan's business in Greenwood Shopping Centre. Despite him being so *totally* out of place. And more totally *not* the kind of guy to chat me up. *So why were you there?*

Because my thoughts were preoccupied with the kind of questions any half-decent telly sleuth would ask herself, and my sleepless night was making me more clumsy than normal, I managed to drop all the change the shop assistant was handing me. Coins scattered over the newspapers piled on the counter, rolled down spaces between them.

'Sorry, sorry.'

The newsagent tutted at my apology. Attended to the queue behind me while I scrabbled for my change. I'd never have seen the second photograph of someone I recognised otherwise. Nearly missed it as it was. Because it was just a little one. Head and shoulders shot. My fifty-pence piece covered it.

But there was no mistaking Dave Griffen's face. He was smiling out, right into my eyes, from the cover of the *Evening Times*:

Attack Leaves Sport's Star Student Critical. Details p. 3

missing links

A Glasgow University science student remains critical in the Western Infirmary following a vicious assault. David Griffen (19), a Scottish Judo Team member, was discovered in Kevingrove Park at 7am this morning.

'I thought he was dead,' said John McLean (45), the dog-walker who found Griffen in undergrowth beside the Kevin Walkway. 'He was unconscious and I couldn't find a pulse. There was blood everywhere.'

Griffen, who remains in a coma, sustained fractures to his skull, arms and legs. Trauma surgeon, Angela Murphy, believes it is 'too soon to rule out the possibility of brain damage.'

A police spokesperson admitted that there is no clear motive for this assault.

'Dave Griffen is a regular student in his second year of biological sciences, who, until recently, also worked as a part-time security guard in a city-centre fashion store. This attack on him appears to be an unprovoked act of violence, inflicted on a popular young man who has never been in trouble. While our investigations are under way we entreat anyone who has seen David Griffen recently or who may have information as to his whereabouts before the attack to come forward.'

The last confirmed sightings of Griffen, before he was discovered, have been provided by fellow students who report seeing him jog from the grounds of Hillview Halls of Residence at 6.15pm yesterday evening. At 6.30 a motorist spotted a male fitting David Griffen's description speaking to the driver of a large black vehicle which pulled up beside him on Maryhill Road.

'If someone saw David after that, please contact the police,' urges Mary Griffen, mother of the student, who is waiting by his bedside. 'There's a missing link somewhere. Someone knows what happened to my son.'

I might know something.

For the umpteenth time since I read the article about poor Dave Griffen –

I saw him recently.

I rang his mobile last night.

Someone else answered.

Does that make me a missing link?

– my hand went to the kitchen phone. Dialled the Police Incident Hotline number from the paper. But quit dialling before the call connected. *You don't know anything for sure. You're always getting stuff wrong.*

Must have gone through the same rigmarole a million times since I blundered home from the newsagent, punch drunk from reading how someone I knew – *Dave . . . who gave me his number . . . Christ . . . this is just like something that happens on the telly . . .*

With my gum tender and raw now the anaesthetic jag had worn off, I couldn't think past my own pain and shock to figure the right thing to do.

So down went the receiver. Into the Maltesers delved my hand.

Comfort. Comfort. Comfort.

Back to the *Evening Times* went my attention, sticky fingers flicking from Dave Griffen's photo to the black and white reality of the horrible *horrible* thing that had happened to him.

Was *still* happening to him.

A great big guy like that. Smart. Fit. Hacked down.

Coma. Broken bones. Blunt weapon.

And his mum, sitting by his bedside. Waiting for him to wake up . . .

I groaned aloud every time I thought about that. Sick to my stomach. OK, too many Maltesers can do that, but to be honest my queasiness started well before I tore into the box I'd bought. And the reason my stomach was churning and cramping and threatening to empty itself from both ends at once had nothing to do with over-indulgence. No. My conscience was poking it, my guts reacting to a truth that my heart didn't want to face:

You *saw Dave Griffen.*

You ***ARE*** *a missing link.*

You should be coming forward.

Admit how close you've been to the poor guy. Literally.

Yeah. You were with Dave Griffen. There when Stefan – your 'boyfriend' by the way, Clod – pinned him to the wall and . . . ***pinned him to the wall*** *and . . . Clod. You were there when Stefan warned Dave Griffen he was a psychopath.'*

There was a second missing link to Dave Griffen.

I was trying not to see it:

'Stefan?'

My whisper tasted sour as I unscrumpled the page I'd nicked from the dentist's. Spread it open next to the *Evening Times.*

'Do you know who I am?' I recalled the grinning, white-tuxedoed smoothie guy in the photograph asking Dave Griffen. Totally in his face.

Totally menacing:

'D'you know you're lucky to be walking out of here?'

My *date* had used those very words to someone whose legs were now broken. Who was possibly brain damaged.

The coincidence – a terrible coincidence – was trying to process itself: Was there any connection between Stefan's threat and Dave Griffen's condition now? Shouldn't I be telling the police my suspicions?

Shouldn't I have told them already?

Please come forward. Any little detail. However small. You were always being invited to do that on *Crimewatch.*

'Better,' I mumbled, hand hovering over the phone again.

But Stefan's photograph stopped me in my tracks. His warm smile. Those dimples. So cute. So decent to me. Even if I wasn't the only female in his life.

He'd be my *ex*-boyfriend if I grassed him up to the police. Sure as I was never going to win *Mastermind* or Miss World he'd be my ex. Forever.

For something he's probably nothing to do with anyway . . .

The longer I stared at Stefan's photograph, honestly, the less I could ever *imagine* his lips coming out with something as nasty as *'Do you know who I am?'* I wondered if I'd misheard what he'd murmured to Dave Griffen. Wasn't Claudia Cloth-Ears the nickname my toad maths teacher liked to use? Didn't I get the wrong end of the stick *all* the time?

Yeah, and if he did blurt that psychopath stuff, I bet it was just hot air. Bragging. Blokes are like that . . .

I nearly convinced myself, remembering how, outside Strut, Stefan had apologised for coming the hard man in front of me. Down on hands and knees. Persuading me he wasn't really the cruel bastard I'd just seen him being . . .

But the spasm in my gut betrayed what I was really

thinking. The Deep Truth, as Georgina would have called it.

Clod, in my head I could hear her: The Voice of Reason. I could even imagine her hand on my wrist. Shaking me lightly, *Pay attention to your gut reaction.*

That's what she'd shrug. End of story. And if I quibbled with her: G, *I think I'm putting two and two together here to get three,* she'd wave the flat of her palm at me.

Clod, you know it's not up to you to decide who's a missing link or not. Just Do the Right Thing: tell the police you met Dave Griffen. And you better mention Stefan turning all Robert de Niro in Strut while you're at it. Plus your phone call to Dave Griffen's mobile. The shouty man. The slapping noises . . . The cops can check if you dialled the right number. And, Clod – Here would be Georgina's most emphatic piece of advice – *No offence, but see before you phone anyone, scribble down what you say. Then you won't go tongue-tied and stammery. In fact, hey! I've a brilliant idea . . .*

mind map

Georgina was *massive* into Mind Mapping. Not for herself. She'd no need, since she was born with one of those cyborg *Total Recall* memories that hoovers every fact and figure and detail of the universe. Then regurgitates it word perfect. There's a special word for that skill. Sounds like 'idiotic' though it's not. That would be me. Shut my eyes once I'd poured my cereal and I wouldn't recall whether I'd Sugar Puffs or Cheerios in my bowl.

That was why Georgina became so keen on me trying strategies that might muscle up my own remedial recall.

Mind Mapping's an easy one, Clod, she encouraged me during that final study leave before I bombed all my exams. *Sheet of paper. Scribble all your main facts. Few words as possible. Bet you'll find things straighten out in your head better. No offence.*

Poor Georgina. She was so uptight I'd end up failing

all the exams I ended up failing, I told her Mind Mapping worked excellently. Liar! Big lazy me used the artist's sketch pad she bought me, not for Mind Map essay planning, but for extravagant Cloddy doodling while I hummed.

Jotted random words. Song lyrics. In three weeks of study leave I mind mapped . . . er . . . let me get out my calculator . . . a total of zero about the Second World War or Romeo and Jools. I was more focussed on the important things in life:

What would Mum be making for dinner? (I'd plot fantasy menus.) Did I feel like a biscuit? (I'd Mind Map all the different varieties I liked, Abernethy to Yo-Yo.)

Reason I did no work? Well I couldn't see the point of putting effort into something I absolutely knew I'd *never* use in the Big Bad World: Hitler's rearmament strategy? The value of x when y is 7? What Willy Shakespeare said ten thousand years ago? Pah: Frigging relevant that tripe, eh?

But here was a weird thing: tonight, with Dave Griffen's nightmare staining my fingertips sweaty newsprint black, I don't know . . . compiling a Mind Map of recent events didn't seem so mind-numbing. How else could I sort my head before I phoned the police? Couldn't exactly ring Australia and launch into details of my possible connection to a promising young science student who was fighting for his life. Mum and Dad had enough on their plate. Why give them long-distance panic? Why double it by telling them about a second guy *I've kinda got involved with, Mumsie?* Who I just so happened to have witnessed threatening this science student you know nothing about . . .

Eventually, all these details were plotted on a new page of my sketch book. Although, funnily enough, just before I started creating my Mind Map, it looked like I might not need to bother. Because I had a phone call.

Stefan?

My heart skipped a beat when I went to answer it. Not quite sure if that reaction was guilt or anticipation. I was in the middle of cutting his photograph from the celeb mag. Spacing it on the other side of a goofy doodle of me. This meant that on my mind map, I was sandwiched between my sweet-talking guy and poor smiley Dave Griffen.

Stefan wasn't the caller though, alas and alack.

'Yo. We've mutual friends, I hear, Quinny. Starsky, Hutch and Big Marge the Curling Cop.'

Never one for *How are you?* timewasting, Uncle Super Mike cut to the chase over a choppy connection.

'You're part of my case, Marge tells me: Operation Marlin. Like that, Quinny? I thought that name up. Biggest fish I've ever gone after, whoever the crazy is behind your dad's place. What a coincidence though, eh? You a witness in this carry-on. Small world. By the way, I think Marge likes you nearly as much as she fancies me! Thinks you'd make a great cop. Must be your big feet.'

Uncle Mike was never one for sweet-talk either. Could be why, at forty-five with all his own teeth, a fancy bungalow, and a Porsche, he'd never reeled in his Mrs Mike. Not that it seemed to bother him.

Oi Grace. Will you leave me be. There are far too many fish in the sea for me to hook a woman, he'd shrug whenever Mum lamented his bachelor status. *Like* literally *too many fish in the sea: herring, salmon, pike. I've no time for a wife.*

I loved him to bits.

'Hey. Are you on your way here now? When? Soon?'

Scissors down, I shouted into Uncle Mike's laugh. Ignoring the way the line hissed back at me, I kept talking. Having someone so solid and near to speak to made me realise how alone I was feeling. I didn't want our conversation to stop.

'Listen,' I prayed Uncle Mike could still hear me. 'There's a guy here. Dave –' I shouted, just as the line cleared totally of static.

'Whhhhat? "A guy called Dave" is it, Quinny? About bloody time.'

Uncle Mike's whistle of approval was so blasting I'd to hold the phone away from my ear. But I could still hear him chuckling. 'And I get the picture, by the way. You're in the middle of a candelit supper and you don't want your old Uncle Mike marching in with a carry-out curry and a six pack to spoil –'

'It's nothing like that,' I interrupted Uncle Mike's frankly ludicrous suggestion. Unfortunately his fantasy had used up the only part of our conversation where the phone reception was decent.

While I tried to put Uncle Mike straight – 'See there's this other guy . . . I sorta kinda know him . . . and he might have something to do with Dave. Dave's been attacked, see. And I'm wondering should I tell the police or . . .'

'. . . a . . . up . . . you . . . What?' Uncle Mike sounded as if he was punching an escape from inside a giant crisp packet full of cellophane gremlins.

'Hello? Listen, I'll just wait till you come. Tell *you* everything instead of the police here. I'd rather do that,' I tried again.

'Quinny, I can't hear . . . word. Are . . . a blanket chewing Dave's face off?'

The way Uncle Mike bellowed reminded me of an old-fashioned recording, volume diluted by distance and time.

'Sorry. Listen, I'll ring off . . . you first thing . . . Dave can have you all to himself tonight. And listen –' Uncle Mike's line cleared again. So did the kidology. 'I don't know if you can hear this, but Marge and the Weegie boys think they've pulled in one of those hammer bams from outside your dad's shop. You OK about doing an ID parade? I'll be with you, Quinny, so don't be worrying –' Uncle Mike's voice shrank. Faded. I just about heard him telling me he was going to try Australia. Find out the latest on baby Sean.

That'll be an expensive waste of calltime, I thought, trying to reach Uncle Mike again. I used landline and mobile, but had no joy. In case he was doing the same to me I stayed close to the phone, ready to grab the receiver.

'I'm going to tell Uncle Mike *everything*. See what he thinks about Stefan,' I promised, my words cutting the silence of the kitchen. So I shivered. Looked over my shoulder, cocking my head and listening for that dreaded snap or creak or scritch and scratch from the other side of a wall that would send me screaming into the night in my bare feet like a wimpy size zero chick from a horror movie.

'Candlelit supper. Aye right!' Hunched over the kitchen table I hugged myself, wondering how I was going to get through another long night when I was already creeped out. That was why I ended up going back to my Mind Map. It was easier to concentrate on that than force myself upstairs to hunch in bug-eyed terror over my books, hearing noises that weren't. I stayed put, working harder than I'd done all year on the page in front of me.

Stefan

I began under the photo from the magazine. Then I added:

AKA Stephen
Mr Josef
Mr Joe

to the first name. 'Why?' I wondered aloud, and then wrote in tiny writing after I bracketed the three aliases, *why does a guy need multiple identities?* A pet name, yeah, like mine: Clod or a tag, maybe: Steve-o was normal.

But four different names? Stefan was Stefan to me, but had been:

Stephen to Lynne in Strut,
Mr Josef to Dave Griffen,
Mr Joe in the magazine.

I plotted all these links before writing:

Dave Griffen

plain and simple beneath the little snap from the evening paper. I drew an arrow, double-headed, from Dave Griffen to Mr Josef. Then connected Dave Griffen to me and wrote down everything I knew about him.

USEFUL FACTS:

DG thought I was a thief in Strut.

Sacked for that (see Stefan).

Threatened by Stefan.

Warned me to watch out for Stefan.

Gave me moby number.

Someone else answered when I phoned. (Man. Foreign??)

Angry. Heard background noises.

Someone getting beat up????

In coma now.

My USEFUL FACTS about Dave Griffen ran almost to the end of the page. Now it was Stefan's turn to have a USEFUL FACTS dossier drawn up about him.

Likes Minstrels

I began, trying to be chronological about the information I listed:

Slight accent. ('British Citizen on passport' he told me)

Two mobile phones. Number dead.

Snake tattoo on left hand (and back – yuk!!!!)

Well-off: loads of credit cards. Sports car, jeepy car???

Student? Chemistry?? (Don't know what uni –

hasn't said)

Studying 'compounds'.

Speaks foreign language: Not French.

Penthouse flat on Clydeside. Don't think he stays

there though.

In business with dad & uncle – 'compounds' . . .

I'd listed so many 'useful' – if vague – facts about Stefan I had to scribble, in tinsy writing, up the side of the page to fit them in. I could hardly read the information in the bottom corner of Stefan's column:

STRUT (where Dave G worked???) Buys a load of designer gear. Regular.

Turned all Tony Soprano with DG.

Scary side.

There was a bit more to add, of course: like Stefan's Park and Bribe system and the furious foreign-language phone conversation he'd taken in Strut that had forced him to end our last date. Plus, I could also mention a certain wad of cash he'd given me before he zoomed out of my life . . .

My pen hovered over the squash of USEFUL FACTS about Stefan. *He doesn't look nearly as sweet on paper as he does in the flesh,* I gulped. Probably the reason I decided not to bother squeezing in a line about Stefan's showing up in the magazine. As Mr Joe. Too depressing, having a supposed-to-be boyfriend add up to something dodgy. The Mind Map wasn't even supposed to *be* about Stefan. I only did it to straighten out what I knew about Dave Griffen.

'You've done that. Bed now. School tomorrow,' I whispered to myself, steeling my nerves.

'Upstairs. Come on! You're knackered.'

29

hidden talent

But have I ever been smart enough to take advice from anyone?

Especially a dumbo like myself.

An hour later I was still at the kitchen table, falsetto-humming through every Beatles song I knew to mask the noise of the empty house. I double-soundproofed by crunching my way through a family packet of Dorritos dipped in peanut butter, while I covered every white space left on my Mind Map with a cartoon.

Note to self: D'you need any formal Art qualifications to be a cartoonist? That's what I was pondering, promising to risk a careers session with Miss Camel-face Connolly and her toilet breath in the morning to find out. *If you don't then maybe all these scenes I've been drawing can be part of my portfolio. They're not half bad. Kinda Manga. Imagine me having a hidden talent?* I was thinking this while I sketched in more fine detail to the best (in my humble opinion) piece of artwork on the page.

Better than my sketch of the hammer attack outside Dad's shop (bloodied window, monobrowed assailant, hyper-dancing accomplice); or my impression of the smoochy booth in the restaurant where Stefan and I had gone on our first date (complete with Radec, the spherical waiter, and the swing combo time-travelled from a 1930s Chicago speakeasy). I sketched Stefan as I'd first seen him in the newsagent's. My hottie on a stick: suede jacket, jeans, shy smile . . .

'Sweet-talking guy,' I hummed under my breath, Mum's brilliant old Chiffon's record playing in my head as I shaded in more tones to the thick flop of hair over his eyes:

'Talking sweet kind of lies,' I drew more definition to his grin. Dotted in his dimple.

'Don't you believe in him, if you do he'll make you cry . . .

He'll send you flowers and paint the town with another girl . . .'

Admiring my completed Mind Map at arm's length, I was singing aloud now.

'Sweeter than sugar, kisses like wine . . .'

Into the eyes of my cartoon Stefan:

'Staaaaaaay away from him . . .

No, you'll never win . . .'

I waggled my finger at the tiny drawing I'd made. Feeling pretty damn chuffed when it was complete. Maybe all those years spent doodling over my jotters hadn't been time wasting after all.

To Uncle Mike.
No hanky panky last night from your little neecee.
Just this masterpiece.
Don't worry, I'll explain everyfing the second I see ya!!
Lotsaluv
Claudia Warhol
Bonsoir.
Au revoir.

I scrawled in massive flourishy writing across the back of my Mind Map since there was no room left on the front.

Feeling very artistic indeed, I left my evening's work propped between two bottles of Bud on the kitchen table so it would attract Uncle Super Mike's attention as soon as he walked into the kitchen. Then I flounced artistically off upstairs to bed.

Wasn't feeling so jittery any more. Was too tired. I'd lost track of all time working on my Mind Map. Couldn't believe my radio alarm was reading the wee small hours already. I'd to double check with the speaking clock. '12.14 a.m.' the fruity-voiced man on the end of the line assured me so pleasantly I snapped back down the receiver, 'Easy for you to say, pal. You don't have double maths first thing,' before I put the phone down.

When it rang out immediately I had one of those insane notions that the speaking clock was live: *Bugger: have I just been rude to some old pensioner trapped in a call centre dishing out timechecks to earn the bread to pay his gas bill?*

I practically apologised to Mr Speaking Clock.

But then a bored-sounding female voice brought me back to the real world.

'Hello. Claudia Quinn, please.'

'Speaking.' I glanced at the time on my bedside alarm again. 12.16.

'Who's this?' *Calling at this hour.*

Could it be Australia? *Something about baby Sean. Mum not up to giving me a message herself. Bad news.*

'Hello, Claudia,' the voice on the end of the line didn't sound Australian.

Nor did it answer my question. Just continued speaking. Kind of automatically. More automatically than the speaking clock man. Like she was reading from a script.

'This is Sister Smith from Intensive Care. Western Infirmary. One of my patients is asking for you.'

'A patient? For me?' I said, but this Sister Smith cracked what sounded like a piece of chewing gum then talked on through me.

'He says you're his friend and he wants to see you. He's very sick so can you come to the hospital, please?'

'But I don't know any . . . Have you phoned the right person? Who is this patient anyway?'

In the pause after my questions I could hear faint

music: female voices, pretty wild-sounding for nurses, if you asked me, out of synch with each other and out of tune with Tom Jones bellowing *It's Not Unusual*.

'Claudia, my patient's waking out of a coma. Could you come to the hospital tonight?' Sister Smith spoke quickly, raising her voice over the background noise. For a nurse she sounded more impatient than caring. Rude, actually, although I supposed working in Intensive Care taught you to cut to the chase in matters that matter. Still. I didn't warm to her attitude.

'So, you'll come and visit now, Claudia?'

There was rustling on the line when Sister Smith was speaking this time. But not crisp leaves interference, like when I was speaking to Uncle Mike. The noises I heard from this call suggested the receiver was being moved about a fair bit. Maybe Sister Smith was multi-tasking: emptying a bedpan, or signalling instructions to another nurse:

Crash cart! Paddles. Stand clear. Charging . . .

But the kind of slidey bumpy muffly rustles I could detect sounded more like the noises you get over the phone when two or more heads are sharing one handset. That's what I half-thought might be going on while I listened to Sister Smith and heard myself naming the only possible person I knew who was in hospital.

'Is the patient Dave Griffen?'

There was nothing but slidey muffly rustles then. I was sure someone was wrestling with the receiver, putting a hand over the mouthpiece.

'Hello?' I raised my voice against whatever tussle was going on down the line.

'Yup.' When Sister Smith did speak again her voice was higher pitched. Her words swallowed and choky-sounding. Like she was smiling or excited or nodding her head, I thought, before I heard her clearing her throat.

'Ahem. Just ask for Intensive Care. Someone'll be looking out for you, don't worry, Claudia,' she said, her voice the sweetest and most friendly it had been throughout the call.

clod's law

You'd have to go back to the Old Testament or *that* scene in *Singin' in the Rain* to find a wetter night for any soul to be trudging in squelching soles through the streets of Glasgow.

Not that there was even a spit when I set out for the Western Infirmary, which explains why I'd no brolly. (Actually I never have a brolly, me.)

The heavens waited till I was a good half way into my journey before they let rip. Clod's Law, eh? And you know that kind of boingy gymnastic rain that buckets so hard it bounces off the pavements soaking you from the bottom up and the top down at the same time? That's what I was up against. I'm not exaggerating, I was so sodden I felt like I'd peed myself. And wet boy-shorts are not the pleasantest of sensations when you're going to meet a fella. Possibly his mum, too. Of course it didn't help that I'd left the house in a denim (the most rain-unfriendly fabric known to man) jacket and *those filthy streetsweeper jeans as* Mum called the trousers that, in fifteen minutes of walking, had blotted up so much puddle-water they were glued to the tops of my thighs like sloppy cold papier mâché.

'Where are all the taxis?' I grumbled, ton-weight legs lurching me along the deserted main road. 'And what am I doing out here anyway? It's the middle of the night.' For the umpteenth time I used my mobile to call a black cab.

'I'm sorry. Your call is in a queue.' The same warm and dry and cheery operator I kept on reaching chimed like it didn't matter that a girl was *drowning* out here. In the background plinky-plonked the same muzac loop of *Here Comes the Sun*. Was that meant to be a joke? Did the cab company play *Let It Snow* in a heatwave?

I couldn't believe my luck: the one and only night I needed to get *anywhere* fast there was barely a car on the road.

Definitely Clod's Law, I sighed, stopping on a corner and squeezing half a gallon of rain from the ends of my hair. For a moment I considered turning back home. Being smart for a change. Phoning the hospital to say I'd pop in first thing in the morning. After all, if Dave Griffen was coming out of his coma he must be less critical now. Delaying my visit a few hours wouldn't matter to him, would it? It might be even for the best, since the sight of a big wet doughball like me appearing at Dave's bedside with her clothes clinging in all the wrong places and her nose running was hardly going to be therapeutic for him, was it?

Yeah, better to come tomorrow on the bus all nice and dry . . .

I was *so* close to aborting my errand-of-mercy. Only I spotted approaching headlights. And wouldn't you know – Clod's sodding Law again – it was *actually* a taxi. No FOR CLOD on its little orange light, alas and alack. No. Just three blootered geezers in the back roaring their heads off at me as the taxi shot past. Sprayed me from head to toe with gutter muck.

'Lovely,' I burbled, attempting to dry my dripping face with my hand. Of course this just made me even wetter. Too wet to turn back. And too late anyway.

Ahead of me, I'd spotted the blurry twinkle of floors in the hospital. Somewhere in those wards stacked on wards was Dave Griffen. Fighting for his life.

But asking for ***me.***

Wow!

The notion of that, I must confess: *Dave Griffen specially asked for me!* is what kept me sloshing the remaining few blocks with ramrods tap dancing on the top of my head, water streaming down my face. I know this sounds mad, and it's embarrassing to admit it. Shallow too. But I actually felt there was something movie-esque about the whole situation: Here I was. The girl in the rom-com. Hurrying, alone through deserted city streets. Plain but strong, I was. Possibly Jennifer Aniston drabbed down or padded up like Renée Zelweger in *Bridget Jones* to play the character of Clod Quinn. An Oscar shoe-in for any female movie star gorgeous enough in real life to go Ugly Betty for a few months. Bulked-up Jen/Ren-as-Clod can hardly see where she's going for all that famous hair (dyed Clod-gingery and back-combed to attain that rain-frizzed look) in her eyes. She stumbles through the wet, half sobbing to herself now when she reaches the hospital. She's banging on locked doors, 'You gotta open up!' trying different entrances, determined to find a way in somehow . . .

Because nothing can stop her. Claudia Quinn's on a mission to revive a friend her heart's telling her could be so much more . . . Can she reach Dave Griffen in time . . .?

Sick this made me sound, I know, but in the throes of hurling my weight against a hospital door that was clearly marked NO ENTRY, I was actually delivering a schmaltzy film-trailer voiceover, muttering under my breath in an American accent. Nearly gave the cleaner dabbing away on the other side a heart attack.

'I need Intensive Care,' I bellowed at him when he spun round to see who was doing all the door-thumping.

'Me'n'all now, thanks very much, hen,' the cleaner was clutching his chest while he peered out at me. 'Way in's round the corner.'

Although there was a locked fire-exit between us, he reeled back when he'd looked me up and down.

'But you'll no' get intae a ward the night.'

Backing away he jerked his mop at me. 'Visiting's seven till eight. Come back tomorrow.'

I'd a doubly helpful exchange with the bloke manning the only open door I could find.

'Looking for Intensive Care –' I made to barge past him, but he blocked my path, legs apart, arms folded. I'd stake my big toe on him being ex-army.

'Where you going, pal?' his greasy brown caterpillar of a moustache rippled when he spoke.

'Intensive Care.'

'That wouldn't be your decision. It'd be mine. Unless you're medically qualified. And the walking wounded always start off in Casualty. That would be here. See that desk. Give your details. Sit. Wait your turn.'

This fella – clearly acting out his Casualty bouncer job as a Glaswegian version of some heavy from *Reservoir Dogs* – strutted me towards a queue in reception. His fingers clamped round the tip of my elbow. Squeezed. Not in a chummy way. In front of me, two stoners with busted noses and bloodied shirts were growling insults through a screen, while the female clerk safe on the opposite side totally blanked them. She just tapped away at a keyboard and smiling to herself like she was being serenaded by Julio Iglesias. Next in the queue a lassie with rubber legs and fairy wings was puking into her tutu. No way was I going near her.

'Look.' One of Uncle Mike's sneaky wrestling jerks freed my arm. I backed away from the Casualty bouncer, checking all round me for direction signs to the wards. 'I'm not sick. Just had a phone call to go to Intensive Care.'

'Zat right. Not sick? But you blow in here shouting the place down?' The doorbloke's tash gave a sarky twitch. 'We'll let the doctors establish your medical fitness, shall we?' he said, the softness in his voice not quite matching the meanness with which he seized my wrist when I dodged past him into a corridor through swing doors marked Wards.

'Backup. Backup.' He followed me, snarling into a walkie-talkie, his request a completely unnecessary waste of hospital resources in my opinion. Single-handedly he made a grand job of pinning me to a wall. Then racking my arm up my back till I yelped at him to stop.

'Don't even think about it on my watch, Wonder-woman,' Casualty bouncer's chewing-gummy breath was a hot whisper on my wet cheek, 'unless,' he was laughing, his caterpillar catching my wet hair in a way that turned my guts, 'you really do fancy a night in Intensive Care with a feeding tube up your nose. Interested?' He leaned his full weight against me. Pushed into my back with his pelvis to make his point. 'Huh?' When he wrenched my wrist all my strength was transfused with pain.

I know this fella was only doing his job, but to say I wasn't happy about the way he restrained me was an understatement. And I knew I was being pretty stroppy but I liked the way he was talking into my ear even less. It was intimate and cruel at once, and worst of all – this is what made me shudder. This is what made me *mad* – it was kinda sleazy: here was a stranger thinking his uniform granted him power and licence to grind himself against me.

Think again, slime-ball.

You wouldn't imagine there'd be any silver linings in growing up to be a girl with size nine feet, but take it from me. See, when you stamp down hard with one of those big plates, it hurts like . . .

'Fuuuuuuu–'

Instantly Casualty bouncer let me go to grab his stomped foot in both hands. While he was dancing the Rumplestiltskin, I used the rear butt-thrust that I'd thought was responsible for opening Stefan's garage to whumph doorbloke to the ground.

Before he was back on his feet, I'd belted through the nearest set of double doors. Up a flight of stairs I stumbled, three at a time.

Six floors later and my heartbeat was thudding out of my ears, though not quite loud enough to drown the furious echo of Casualty bouncer's promises about what I'd be getting when he'd his hands round my neck.

I'd be lying if I didn't admit I was scared. Metaphorically speaking this bampot chasing me had me up against a wall. He was in his rights to do so too. And I only had one option:

Keep on climbing, Clod. Find Sister Smith. Sort everything out . . .

Rubber-legged, totally whacked, I burst through the doors of Intensive Care with so much force that they walloped the walls they were hanging from like fire-crackers exploding. Then ricocheted back. Whammed into my face.

When I took my hands away from my pulped nose and saw the evil eye I was getting from the nurse who'd responded to my entrance, I decided Casualty bouncer was a mere pussy cat.

'Can you read?'

He might have had the build of a malnourished whippet and the hissiest of whispers, but this guy in a white tunic was no Sugar Plum Fairy.

'NO ENTRY to my ward.' He flourished the back of his hand against the warning signs in the ward doorway. Made the same gesture at the SILENCE posters flanking the walls. And it *was* his ward. He'd the badge on his tunic flashed in my face to prove it:

HEAD OF ICU: MARTIN SMART.

'Sister Smith. I've to ask for Sister Smith. She phoned,' I gasped, blood from my nose streaming into my mouth.

'Ssssh,' Nurse Smart's index finger was pressed so firmly to his lips that their flesh paled. 'You're not shouting across to your pals in a nightclub now, sweetheart,' Martin Smart half-shooed, half-backed me from the ward entrance just as Casualty bouncer's latest threat echoed up from the stairwell below.

'See when I get my hands on you –'

'Sensational. A security ding-dong's *just* what vulnerable patients on life-support need at one o'clock in the morning,' Martin Smart's tone was caustic enough to strip paint. 'But it's not happening here.' As he spoke, Martin Smart was flipping down a bolt on the ward door, closing the other door on me, flapping me backwards.

'Don't you even think about crashing my ward looking for trouble. Or turning physical on me. Just get explaining yourself. Before I wheech you down the service lift to meet the big hospital cop who stops lollies like you stopping me from doing my job.'

Now I was really scared.

'Please. I'm not looking for trouble. But I was phoned to come here. Urgently. By a nurse. From here.

Honest,' I clasped my hands before the flinty eyes of Martin Smart. 'Sister Smith called from Intensive Care. Said Dave Griffin was asking for me. Now that guy out there's gonna kill me –'

'Right. Zip the lip two secs now.' Martin Smart, who listened hand on hip to my burbling, suddenly whisked me back through the door of his ICU and bolted it with a fraction of time to spare before Casualty bouncer set about pummelling it instead of me.

The tongue-lashing he took from Martin Smart for that!

'You *dare* stress my patients. There's folk hanging on to life by a thread in here. I'm getting right on to your supervisor –'

I pressed myself against a wall behind the ward door, listening to Martin Smart's whisper grate strips off Casualty bouncer through the crack in his ward doors. I tried to pinch my nosebleed away while all this was going on. Tried not to sob, but when I finally heard the bouncer's footsteps receding down the stairwell, I dissolved. Slid down to the floor, a streak of rain and tears and blood.

'Now this better be good, because I've put hospital security on the line for you, but you look like you're telling me the truth, and I hate bullies.'

Still whispering, but not quite so harshly, Martin Smart beckoned me to my feet. Led me into a washroom. I waited while he scrubbed his hands with antiseptic soap, then nodded for me to do the same.

'You said a Sister Smith phoned?' he pressed paper towels to my nose, pursing at me in the mirror. 'Not from this hospital.' He shook his head. 'What's your name, princess?'

'Dodia.' I met Martin Smart's eyes above the sink. Could tell by the way he was frowning that, at least, thank goodness, he definitely believed my reason for being here.

'A Dizder Smid pode be,' I added. Not particularly helpfully.

'Two secs, Dodie,' Martin Smart said, guiding my hand to my nose. 'Keep pressing. Head up.'

I thought he might have gone to find ice but he came back empty-handed. There was an elderly female nurse with him.

'Right. Nurse Young here's worked thirty years on this ward. Doesn't know your Sister Smith.'

'Sorry,' Sister Young shrugged at me. 'And I've just checked the rosters in case there's an agency nurse started but –'

'Don't know what this is about, Dodie. Something fishy. No Sister Smith in the Southern General either. We've just phoned –'

Martin Smart paused to ease the paper towel from my nose. He wetted fresh ones to wipe round my cheeks and mouth and eyes. Then he manoeuvred me to a chair and sat me gently on it. Tilted his chin to squint down like he didn't know what to make of anything I'd told him so far.

'We transferred David Griffen there this morning. Showed signs of waking up, didn't he, Gloria?'

'Squeezed Mum's hand when she spoke to him,' Nurse Young's voice was choky as she blew her nose on the paper towel Martin Smart flicked at her. He gave me his first smile when he said, 'Would you look at Gloria? Nursing's biggest softy. Your friend's stable enough for a neuro ward now, though –'

'And did he speak? See Sister Smith phoned because Dave was asking for me –' I interrupted. Over my head Martin Smart and Nurse Young exchanged a look.

'Is David a special friend?' Martin Smart wasn't meeting my eyes. 'His mum never mentioned a girlfriend –'

OK. I know when it comes to sussing people out I'm not exactly high functioning, but I'd say that the way Martin Smart's voice had softened meant . . .

Well, I knew he was consoling me. Because basically the next stuff he said about Dave Griffen was preparing me for the worst. Not that I made full sense of everything. What I learned about Dave Griffen only began to sink in while I slumped, eyes closed, head pressed hard against the steel wall opposite Nurse Young in a service lift that led me out the hospital through an unmanned exit.

Dave Griffen's body was on the mend.

He was stable now.

But he certainly hadn't asked for me.

'No way, Dodie,' Martin Smart had actually taken my hand to explain.

Because Dave couldn't speak. No chance.

Too many tubes in his mouth even if he could.

Not to mention wires holding his jaw in place.

And he was being kept under sedation while his brain was still swollen.

His parents the only visitors he was allowed.

'So, listen, whoever dragged you out here tonight is sicker than the patients in my ICU, sweetheart. And that's saying something.' Martin Smart had narrowed his eyes as he walked me to the lift, handing over a hospital issue personal effects bag containing my wet clothes.

'The scrubs suit her, don't they, Gloria?' Like my personal stylist he drew his hand down the length of me in my greens as the lift door closed on me and Nurse Young.

'You take care,' I heard Martin Smart whisper.

sleepwalking

'You take care.'

What a coincidence. I remembered being told that by Dave Griffen himself. Last time we met.

Georgina too.

Way more recently. Although, since I'd been belting out my bedroom for the hospital when her *War and Peace*-length email pinged into my Inbox, I'd only allowed myself to glance at the first few lines she'd written:

> C, Sorry, but I don't like the sound of your Stefan guy. What you've told me about him reminds me of that line from Hamlet's stepfather smiling and smiling and being a villain? You take care. I mean it.

I'd read and left it at that.

I'll tackle her Shakespeare quotes over tea and toast

once I'm hot showered and in my jammies . . .

That was the cosy prospect just about keeping my spirits up and no more as I left the hospital via the Soiled Laundry And Dead Body Exit and set off home. Honestly, I'd never known such a dreich night. You wouldn't even put your bin out in it. The streets were still deserted and it was as wet as ever although the rain, wouldn't you know, had changed into thick, whirling sleet in the half hour since I'd been tricked into Intensive Care to visit a guy in a coma who'd upped sticks . . .

'This just isn't funny!' With the thin scrubs I'd changed into soaked through already and plastered to me like an icy second skin, I wore the bag holding my other wet clothes on my head while I rang for a cab again.

'I'm sorry, all our operators are busy at the . . .' the same toasty voice lulled before I silenced it with one of those phrases you just *have* to use sometimes even though mothers like mine claim there's *never* an excuse for filth from the well-raised civilised girl I'm supposed to be.

Well I don't feel very bloody civilised tonight, Mumsie, I thought, suddenly *aching* to see Mum driving towards me right now, saving me from this horrible night.

And no matter what time it is. Even if you're in bed already, I just press a few buttons on my phone and hey presto . . .

'Ooops.'

The money-wasting text I sent without knowing I'd done it:

SOS. stranded. Come get me
Ma?

has to qualify as one of the most pointless act of my life. Stoopid girl here had so much water on the brain I was fantasising Mum half a block, not half a world away. Peeping her horn to mortify me, waving dementedly through the windscreen as she slowed down, leaning over to kiss me as soon as I threw my carcass into the seat beside her and automatically turned down her Will Young CD. *Would you look at the state of you?* Mum'd be gasping, pretending to be affronted. I'd be breathing in her perfume, rubbing away the trace of her lipgloss on my cheeks.

And if Mum was here, I thought turning a corner, away from the well-lit grounds of the hospital, *no way would I be taking this skanky walkway to the main road.* It was so dark, I literally couldn't see the ground in front of me. Had to shuffle along in case I tripped over some junkie or shopping trolley or waterproof murderer or something. That made me tense, made me clench my mobile in my fist, start humming at the darkness. *Eye of the Tiger,* high and growly.

So, compared to the noise I was making, the sawing cellos of my *I Am the Walrus* ringtone sounded positively ladylike. The way I answered my phone wasn't:

'Who's this? Sister bloody Smith?'

'Babes, guess who?'

The voice, the last voice in the *world* I was expecting, stopped me dead. Dead in the middle of a puddle. So deep that water lapped over the rims of my shoes. I suppose that was why my teeth chattered when I tried to speak:

'St . . . St . . . Stefan?'

'Didn't I promise to phone? Long time no hear, eh, Claudia?' his voice gave a chuckle. 'So what's my babes up to, then? You sound a bit uptight.'

As I've hinted more than once, yours truly has never been a megawatt in the bright lights department; I'm more your eco-friendly bulb. The kind that take an hour and a half to do what they're meant to. Stupid sometimes, in other words.

But not dumb.

At least, that's what I reckoned when, alone in the middle of this pitch dark walkway, shin-deep in a puddle, I calculated with the speed of a mathematical prodigy that I definitely wasn't dumb enough to tell snake-tattooed Stefan, with his heart of a psychopath, multiple indentities and an Honours Degree In Threatening The Life Out Of Muscle-bound Blokes like Dave Griffen, my exact whereabouts.

Wasn't I only *here* because of a certain Muscle-bound Bloke?

Might not go down too well with his competition. So I lied. Gave Stefan a lion-sized yawn.

'I'm in bed actually.'

'In bed? You mean I've spoiled your beauty sleep? Oh, babes.'

Stefan's reply was soft as a purr. However I heard him so clearly his lips might have been touching my ear. And a shiver ran the length of me.

'Where are *you*?'

My words bounced back hollow off the high concrete walls flanking the walkway. The echo my question had created jittered around me so that instinct made me turn. On edge. Panicked. Checking over my shoulder. Head right. Then left, eyes peering into the gloom to the end of the walkway. Ears straining beyond the tap tap tap of sleet-fall. *Just to check,* I gulped, *that there isn't someone stalking me. Creeping through the walkway. Closing in. Ready to pounce.*

'Don't worry, babes . . .'

It took as long for me to realise that the voice coming through the phone was also coming towards me as it did for me to separate Stefan's silhoutette from the charcoal murk of the walkway. He seemed to belong to the very night itself.

'. . . and don't sound so nervous. It's only me,'

Stefan's voice murmured into both my ears at once, the faint light from his mobile revealing his perfect smile to me for the first time in days.

'Fancy meeting you here. Sleepwalking, are you?' he said, voice soft as chocolate melted over a low heat, although the gloved hand grasping mine and taking my mobile away tightened round my fingers meaner than Neil's used to do when we played chicken. More in shock than pain, I gasped (So much shock that I dropped the hospital bag holding my wet clothes. Plop. I heard it meet the puddle I was standing in). Unable to wrench my hand free before Stefan's arm was hooking my neck, I felt his leather sleeve creak against my nose as he jerked me closer and closer to his side until I was completely off balance, one leg clear of the puddle where my clothes floated away. Now my entire weight was propped against the length of Stefan's flank.

'Imagine you telling me porky pies, babes. Let's go,' he tutted, a yank to my neck stumbling me towards the end of the walkway. A car pulled up across the exit as we approached. No headlights, engine running. A man: burly, squat, his lower face scarfed, held the rear door open until Stefan reached it. Muttered something foreign. Stefan's voice sounded guttural and low, older than the one I knew, and whatever he said ended in a rough chuckle and made the burly man step back into the yellow glow of the first decent streetlight since the hospital, whipping the scarf from his face. In the moment before this man came round the back of me and wrapped his scarf over my mouth – jerking back my neck. Jerking harder to tie his knots. Grunting with the effort he was putting into his task – I glimpsed his upper features. By the time he and Stefan were humphing me on to the back seat of the car, using their knees to shove me inside when I started to struggle, I remembered where I'd seen those eyes before. That monobrow.

I was being manhandled by the hammer guy.

sugarcoated

. . . Who drove like he hammered. Hard. Purposefully. Not one of those motorists to be sidetracked by distractions like traffic lights, weather conditions, speed cameras, sharp bend signs, give ways, or STOP warnings. No. No. No. Once Hammer Man had strapped my wrists to the grab handle in the back of the car with some kind of impossible-to-wriggle-out-of cheese-wire, then rearranged his stale-tobacco flavoured scarf so tightly across my mouth that I couldn't swallow, he moseyed round to the driving seat. Without a word spoken. And put his foot down.

'Sorry about all this. Don't worry; it's going to be over soon.' Stefan's voice was melted chocolate again. His gloved fingertip, stroking free a strand of hair trapped in my gag, was more delicate than the footsteps of a ladybird tiptoeing across my eyebrows.

Bastard I recoiled, my confusion at Stefan's

sugarcoated kidnap tactics making me almost too angry to be seriously scared . . . yet.

He was messing bigtime with my head, his bitter sweetness worse than any direct cruelty.

He still seems so kind, I was thinking while my eyes goggled over the top of my gag at Stefan. *Though he's keeping me trussed. Choking in the back of a car that has to be stolen.* ***Has*** *to be. Otherwise Hammer Man wouldn't be tripping every speed camera we fly past.*

'Listen gonna just let me go,' I tried to plead, but all I could manage was a gargle, dry and ugly, the half-swallow of it bringing tears to my lashes.

'Sorry, babes?' Stefan leaned his face against mine. Cheek to cheek we were. Mine wet, his sweet-cologned.

'I didn't catch that. You want something?'

His finger slid down my face to the edge of the gag, hooking it away from my mouth just enough for me to be able to talk. Couldn't though. As soon as I closed my lips and licked them, the saliva that rushed my parched throat set me hacking and retching.

'Claudia.'

Tut-tutting, Stefan pinged the scarf back against

my mouth. His mouth was sour.

'Didn't that polite mum you bored me to death about teach you to cover your mouth when you cough?' He pouted at me. Leaned close to whisper, 'Hospitals are filthy places, too. Who knows *what* nasty germs you've picked up visiting your sick friend. You should be keeping them to yourself, babes. Though you're not exactly good at keeping anything to yourself. Are you? Eh?' The finger of Stefan's glove switched under my nose like a playful kitty-tail.

'No good at all. Big feet, big nose, big butt, big boobs, big mouth. I should have known that.' His smile remained, though the words behind it hardened as he called out to Hammer Man, 'Hear what I'm telling our *problem,* Len?'

Stefan kept his eyes twinking on mine as he patted hammer guy's shoulder. Whatever comment he translated made Len suck air through his teeth and ignore the corner he was aquaplaning to glare at me. Then he and Stefan chuckled. It wasn't a jolly-Santa sound.

'Hey, by the way, babes. Case I forget,' Stefan's

voice was light as candyfloss again, almost a simper, 'How *is* your other boyfriend? Sitting up in bed is he? Eating grapes? Hey. Hey. Calm down, babes –'

Soon as Stefan asked about Dave Griffen like that: Throwaway. Mocking. Well, I know given my circumstances I'd have been wise to sit tight, but I completely lost it. Couldn't help myself.

'What d'you know about Dave? Did you attack him? Was it you who sent me to visit him? *That* was sick!' I screamed through my gag while I thrashed and bucked and kicked out at Stefan heedless – at least for the first few seconds – that the slightest movement I made slit the cheese-wire through my wrists like they were the Cheddar it was designed to slice.

Stefan eventually pointed out the damage I was inflicting on myself. 'Ooooh, your poor handies, babes.' He flapped at me to sit still. 'You're bleeding everywhere, and I really hate the sight of blood,' he winced, adding, as he shifted away from me on the back seat, 'leaves too much information.' While I was distracted by the cold tone of this comment, he grabbed my ankles. Crossed them over so I couldn't kick out any more then pinned them together under the weight of his thighs.

'Y'know those cuts are going to sting like mad. Try to keep calm. Here, is this better?' As one hand soothed my shin in a circle, Stefan's other reached across me. Yanked the scarf down over my chin.

'Who are you? What did you do to Dave? Why are you doing this to me?' Still writhing to free myself from Stefan's pin-down, all my questions spluttered out at once. Though I was beginning to lose strength now: the adrenalin rush of my capture giving way to the raw pain throbbing into my wrists as blood trickled warm up the drenched sleeves of my scrubs.

An even deeper pain splintered the base of my spine where my legs lay twisted under Stefan at right angles to my body. When I tried to choke back a sob I betrayed myself, the spill of hot tears leaving me slumped against the car seat.

'Oh babes, don't be so upset.' Stefan used the back of his glove to wipe my eyes. 'I really *am* sorry about all this. It's nothing personal, but the bottom line is you've caused me too much hassle. Now you're a risk I can't afford. Business is business, after all.' I caught the scent of fine cologne mingled with good leather as Stefan's hand smoothed my hair back from my face. His touch dragged against my wet skin.

'All a bit of a shame, coz I thought you were the smartest, babes. Remember how you lied? When we met? Told me you saw nothing from your dad's window? Oh babes.' The fingers of Stefan's glove blew me an admiring kiss. 'That was impressive. See,' he tilted my chin up so I had to look him in the eye. 'I'd been watching Len here. Len and Janek. He's my cousin, by the way. Couldn't be here tonight, though he'd have enjoyed this very much. Poor Janek's in a police cell. Because . . .' Without looking away from me, without interrupting what he was saying, Stefan used his index finger to put strain on the cheese-wire. It *really* hurt. '. . . some blabbermouth babes told her police chums she recognised him. Oh dear, Claudia. Now we *both* end up here.'

Stefan flopped his head back against the seat rest, rolled it from side to side, his eyes closed, his voice flat.

'Turns out I was wrong about you. You *are* dimmer

than you look, babes. If only you'd turned a blind eye in daddy's shop when Janek and Len here were sorting a bit of business out for me. Nothing to do with you, was it? Eh? My people having a word with one of my competitors. Clearing up a few private matters. Firm to firm . . . Ahhh . . . But it's all too late now.' Stefan swept a weary hand from the ties at my wrist, then to the back of Len's head. He shrugged. Sighed. Waggled my mobile phone at me. 'I had great hopes that none of this . . .'

'None of what?' I gulped, little-girl-lost panic in my voice betraying my rising terror. *What's this guy going to do with me?* Stefan didn't answer. Just kept shaking his head. Eyes still closed, he tapped the side of his nose with my mobile. The gesture was another of his promises: *That's for me to know and you to find out.*

There was silence in the car then, broken only by the swish of wheels on puddly gravel and the noiseless screaming in my head: *You're totally trapped here. Finished.* I gasped aloud then, plunging cramp griping my stomach so viciously as my guts turned to liquid fear my arms automatically dropped to clamp the pain.

With tethered hands, this was my most stupid move yet. The cheese-wire bit so deeply I arched up in my seat, groaning right into Stefan's ear. Neither he nor Len gave any sign they were aware of my distress. Both ignored me, Len's eyes fixed on the road, Stefan's shut. Expression blank. He seemed totally composed. Brow smooth. Faint smile on his lips. Relaxed, like he was meditating or something.

Didn't even seem to register the shrill of my mobile in his hand when my Inbox beeped.

'Hey.' Stefan let several moments pass before frowning into my phone screen. 'Who could be texting my babes at this late hour? Interrupting her beauty sleep again. Could it be the new boyfriend, eh?' he asked, making a panto of shifting to cosy beside me again till our shoulders touched.

'Hel – lo Clau-dia. Duh! Sorry I can't talk too good no more,' he monotoned, attempting – dreadfully – a dumbo, Arnie-Robocop voice.

As he opened my Inbox, he was nudging me.

'Have I guessed right? Is it dead brain Daaaaave?' he nudged me harder. Then whistled. 'No! But guess who? It's Mumsie, babes. Oooooh.' Like a selfish kid keeping a toy to himself, Stefan angled the screen away from me so I couldn't read Mum's message. He scrambled what he saw into a trilly falsetto nonsense: 'Yah, yah, wah, wah.' Then he showed me the screen, used the same silly voice to read it aloud. It made him laugh. Not me. He sounded nothing like Mum when she's off on one and his mimicry of her sickened me:

> 'Where r u Cloddy? Why
> stranded? Where?'

he primped,

> 'Iv called Uncle Mike to help u.
> Fone him. Not been clubbing
> have u? Hope not. Uv school!!!
> Baby Sean fab. C pic??? Perfect.
> Dad flying home 2 days. Me
> next week. Can't wait 2 c U
> pet. Love u lots. Mum xxxx.

Oh dear. How sad. Never mind.'

Stefan, dropping the falsetto, sing-songed into the mobile without looking up. In the flattest of voices he added, 'Your mumsie's going to be too late.' He scrolled the functions on my phone as he spoke.

'Aha,' he grinned, flashing the screen at me long enough to catch the blur of a tiny face, its eyes scrunched tighter to the world than the clenched fists below them.

'Dere's Aunty Claudia's little sick boy. How come all de little boys you know are sick, babes? Do you make dem sick maybe?' Stefan said in a baby voice, deleting what was on the screen even though I was still devouring the first picture of my first nephew . . . *Maybe the last picture I'll see of him . . .*

'Ringtones. You won't be needing to change yours again. Isn't that a thought,' Stefan said, voice back to normal as he ran through my Functions menu again.

'Messages? Nope. Not yet . . . Ah here we are: Camera. Say cheese, babes.'

Before I knew what Stefan was doing he'd whisked my gag back over my mouth then stretched his arm close to my face. Snapped a photo of me, chuckling as he leaned over the front seat to show the result to Len.

'Just saying, I've seen you looking better. Though not a lot,' he translated the remark that Len's shoulders were still enjoying. 'But you know what, babes? This time tomorrow, ugly as you are, your mum's going to treasure this last piccy more than *anything*. I promise. Isn't that a comforting thought? And your face is going to be in all the papers. Hows about that? You'll be famous . . . *IN*famous,' he nodded, busy with the phone again. Disregarding the beep of at least two incoming messages. *Mum? Uncle Mike?* Busy texting his own.

'There. Message sent back to Mumsie. Want to hear your farewell, babes?'

Despite me shaking my head, humming to drown Stefan's cruelty – *Ugly* he called me. *Bastard. Liar. Psychopath* – he went on, his voice mocking me now. Slowly he monotoned: '*"I blabbed, stupid me. Love from Cloddy x x x."* How's that. All the way to Australia. With your last ever piccy. Techonology nowadays. "Fab" as your mum might say.'

Stefan was rolling his eyes, lashes girlishly a-flutter

as he opened the back of my phone, pocketing my SIM card. He lounged across me to reach the window button, droning 'Beeeeeeep' while it slid open. He hurled the two sections of my mobile into the sleet.

'Bye bye Mummy and Daddy. Beeeeep,' he waved as he put the window back up.

Len was braking for the first time in the entire journey, the car bumping over soft, uneven ground. *We're on the Clydeside,* I realised, when Len drove past a reflected chain of golden lights bobbing on black river-water.

The image was so beautiful it stabbed my heart.

The car was slowing to a crawl before a massive gate with barbed wire at the top. When Stefan clicked a button on the remote control he pulled from his coat pocket the gate shuddered open, though Len didn't wait till it clunked wide enough for his wing mirrors to survive before he floored the car though it. Weaving like Dick Dastardly in and out of a settlement of freight containers, he drove at the only one with its door gaping and its ramp lowered. The car felt like a plane engine thrusting into reverse on a short runway when it finally drove into the container and stopped.

'Ultimate destination, babes,' Stefan chimed, in what I assume was his version of a film-trailer voice. As he spoke, he snapped his gloved fingers over Len's shoulder, palm upturning to receive the kind of scary blade the police always display on the news when they're having a knife amnesty.

'Now,' Stefan said, lunging at me.

'No, no, no,' he laughed as I shrank so desperately against the door of the car that the facing creaked. 'Remember I hate blood. Just making you more comfortable. I never get my hands dirty.'

Stefan's face was a fraction from mine, close enough for him to land me a peck on the nose as his knife freed my wrists with a single swipe.

'Much better,' he said, sawing the individual knots on each hand. When my arms dropped dead and rubbery on to his lap he massaged the life back into my fingers. Because they were too numb for me to wrench away, I had to let sit there and let him stroke me, his voice as gentle as his touch when he murmured, 'Babes, you've made such a mess of yourself already.

Spoiling Len's fun. He won't like that . . .'

Stefan was out the car while this detail about his henchman was sinking in. He was pulling his gloves off, balling them. Flinging them over his shoulder into the recesses of the container. Next he shucked off his leather coat, stepping over it, then twitching adjustments to the shirt cuffs peeking from the sleeves of the business suit he was wearing underneath. From its breast pocket he slipped out a pair of tinted specs. They were dark. Heavy-framed. Way too old for him.

'Quinn Family Eyecare, no less,' he said. 'Christ, your dad tells some criminal jokes. No wonder you look so pissed off, stuck behind that desk, babes, hearing patter like that. He sells some vile gear too. Eh, babes?' Stefan waggled the arms of his specs, blinked over the top of the frame, acting the goof.

'Look as swotty as the chemical researcher I'm meant to be, don't I?' he leaned into the car to ask. *Reading my mind.*

'Stephen Alan. PhD. University of Strathclyde. Pleased to meet you,' he said, offering me a handshake which I didn't accept.

'Suit yourself,' he shrugged, opening a clear plastic wallet Len handed him. Apart from the plane ticket which Stefan slipped into his jacket pocket there must have been at least a dozen passports: European. American. Australian . . . Stefan sifted them, flicking to the photographs on the back, discarding each one by throwing it over his shoulder to where he'd chucked his gloves until there were only two passports left.

'There's the Comic Optician himself.' Stefan leaned on the car door to flash me Dad's missing passport.

When I tried to grab it from him – 'You stole that. And you nicked Dad's VISA too, didn't you? That time you went into the bedroom. You scummy . . .' Stefan just nodded at Len, eyebrows raised.

'Hey, the bitch is catching on. She's all yours, but remember . . .' Before Stefan turned his back saying something to Len I didn't understand, he tapped his watch with an impatient finger. One swift cock of his head was enough to direct Len to lunge at me. Seizing my wrists, he whipped me from the car so fast I spun round on my heels, staggering backwards.

When my rear end landed on the metal floor of the

container, the force of my fall clanged like a distress bell.

'Ooops-a-daisy, clumsy clogs.'

Stefan's words were only just audible and no more over the reverberation I'd caused. His own footsteps echoed through the container as he walked towards its unlit rear, swallowed in the dark beyond the apron of light from the car headlights.

'Anyway, I'll be getting out Len's way. Goodbye, babes.' Stefan was sniffing crocodile tears. 'Was *ever* so sweet while it lasted,' I heard him mock before a car door slammed and an ignition kicked over and a pair of reverse lights pricked the black recesses of the container. Their zig-zag approach to within a few centimetres of the floor where I sat didn't distract Len. Hauling me to me feet, he roped my waist then my upper arms to a rusty ring hanging from the container roof. When I was hoisted off the ground till only my toes scuffed the floor and no more, Len gagged me with his scarf again, the effort of tightening it over my mouth making him grunt. Meanwhile, Stefan eased past us in one of those tiny Smart cars. His vision, as he reversed, was fixed, not on me, or Len, but on his rear-view mirror. *Like I'm not even here.* Just as I was thinking this, the lenses in Stefan's specs caught a reflection from Len's parking light. They glinted red and blank on me. *Like there are no eyes behind them. No windows to the soul,* I thought, trying to peer past the dark tint.

Plead with all my heart for my life.

But Stefan sat in his car. He watched me. Me and hammer man.

Like he must have been watching us both that day of the attack outside Dad's shop. When this all started . . .

this is it . . .

Hammer man takes his time. Humphing items from the boot of his car. Doesn't say a word. Not a one. Doesn't look at me either, and here I am: wriggling and straining. Grunting to free myself. My eyes begging at him. At Stefan in the car outside: *Please don't do this to me. Or my mum. My dad.*

A lamp appears first. Weird, I think when I see it. It's the exact same as one Neil bought Dad three Christmases ago.

Call that a present! I'd slagged it when Dad unwrapped what's basically a bulb inside a red plastic cage. Great big long rat's tail of an extension cable on it.

Now I'm seeing Len's portable lamp and thinking how, every time Dad uses his, he proclaims it the *Best present anyone's ever given me.* It's bizarre seeing something that's innocent and practical and *good* in my dad's hands being put to use by someone like Len. His version of Dad's lamp plugs into the cigarette lighter hole on the dashboard of the car that drove me here. Switched on, a pool of sick yellow brightness floods from it, picking out all these rusty brown suspicious-looking stains on the area of the container floor where I'm tied.

The stains make me think about those girls. The foreign ones Starsky and Hutch showed me: Tortured. Murdered. *Did they die in here too? At Len's hand? Stefan looking on?* I gulp, looking wildly around this miserable container. That's when I notice, through the open rear door of the car that brought me here, dozens of black-red bloodstreaks. Mine, these are. From my sliced wrists. Soiling the pale leather upholstery. Can't help staring at them while Len moves back and forth from me to the boot of the car. He still ignores me, even when I thrash out my dangling legs and manage to kick over a plastic petrol canister he places within range of my size nines. When it falls over – Oh, Mammy-Daddy! Sloshing with fuel – Stefan parps his horn alerting Len who pauses on his way to the boot again. Rights the canister before producing a toolbox.

Coincidentally Dad's got one of them too. Exact same gunmetal grey colour. Rusty round the base. Pulls out in tiers like a fancy box of chocolates with a hidden layer underneath. Dad keeps old fuses and useless bits of flex and Christmas fairy light spares in the sump of his toolbox. Len has screwtop jars, same as the ones Dad crams with old nails he'll never use. Len's jars have pills in them though. Two-tone capsules. Pretty colour combinations: lime and crimson, violet and grey. He has to lift some of the jars out before he can dig down for a bunch of syringes. He picks one, holds it between his teeth while he's opening the nearest of the lidded compartments at the top of his toolbox. Think it's the drawer Dad keeps for screwdrivers. Len's is crammed with glass vials. They tinkle when his fingers disturb them.

I'm thinking what a sweet sound even while I'm panic-gasping behind my gag. Humming through my nose. *Amazing Grace.* Mum's song. Mum's prayer. Loud as I can. The noise has no effect whatsoever on Len. His monobrow is a dipped V of concentration. Syringe in hand, he's drawing the contents of the upturned vial into its needle. Even when I hum higher, tuneless, desperate, he works away, not a glance in my direction.

Me? When Len holds the filled syringe up to Stefan, and Stefan's blank-eyed head nods *carry on*, my eyes are bulging out their sockets. Moving in close to me, Len flicks a fingernail against the syringe. Just like they do on *ER*, *Casualty*, *House*. Checking for air bubbles before the needle goes in. I'm bucking at the ring tying me to the container ceiling, every ounce of my strength working to tear my body free. But Len puts a stop to that. Syringe clamped between his teeth again he crushes his side against my ribcage, pinning me to the container wall, his full bulk waiting till I stop fighting.

And the moment I'm still, he presses his hand to the side of my face, twisting my jaw. Out the corner of my eye I see the tip of the needle closing in on my neck. Stefan in the background, making sure Len does what he's paid for.

Bastard.

Whatever poison's in that syringe it hits me from the feet up, a rush numbing my knees so fast that by the time I realise they're paralysed I'm sagged into Len, head lolling on to his shoulder. Drooling. I'm so drained of voluntary movement that when he steps back from me, my unsupported jaw cracks my collar-bone so my teeth pierce my tongue. Ignoring my yelp, Len drops the syringe into the toolbox, closes up the lid then leaves the container. My eyelids, dragging heavier than the dead weight of my roped body, try to track Len's movements but I can't turn my head any more. Just hear the sound of the toolbox dropping into a car-boot before it's closed. Then the grind of metal moving. Slam. One of the container doors has been shut, halving the light beaming in from Stefan's car. He's revving its engine as Len returns to where I'm sagged from my rope like a wasted rag doll.

All the time trying to make my mouth work.

Trying to beg: *Please let me go.*

But all I can do is watch and follow Len's hands through a slit in my drugged eyes while he opens the petrol canister. Sloshes its contents freely across the car before discarding the canister at my feet so fuel hits my hair, my clothes, my face. From the dashboard, Len yanks out the flex of the portable light, plunging my surroundings into virtual darkness.

In the distance of the night, and just for a moment, I hear a duet of sirens before Len's drowning them out with whistling and pom-pom-pomming. *Same as Dad when he's reaching the end of a trickly repair job,* I can't help thinking. And thinking about Dad makes me see him in my mind's eye: plump and bumbly and harmless, his reading specs – or Mum's more likely – tipping squinty off his nose while he works.

Am I ever going to see my dad again? Or Mum? Georgina . . .? I'm screaming out my dumb, paralysed mouth, the voice in my head as high pitched as those caterwauling sirens I can still hear, so near but yet too far, somewhere out there in a Glasgow night.

What are you doing? Please stop. Please don't leave me here, I want to gurgle but Len's outside the container now, interrupting his job-done whistling to call something to Stefan. Probably *Mission Accomplished.* Whatever, it makes Stefan flat his hand to his horn and his foot to the floor of his car.

Then Stefan and Len are off their mark, the second

door of the container slammed and locked while the burning ball of rags that's kicked into the container rolls towards me. Flames leap so quickly from it that I can see them dance and grow through the skin of my leaden eyelids and I can smell scorched cloth. Paint melting.

Petrol.

So this is it.

The container swirling with smoke. Any air coming into my nose bitter and foul and thick.

Strangely enough, although I'm panicking, struggling to breathe, knowing that the flames licking the interior of the car, burning away my bloodstains and Len's fingerprints, are reaching out for me already, part of my brain – probably for the first time in its seventeen years of being wired to me – is clear and racing.

Stefan can't get away with this. ***Won't*** *get away with it. I've left a trail,* I realise, my thoughts flashing from the email I'd sent Georgina sitting in my Sent box to the bag of clothes in the hospital alley and my Mind Map ready for Uncle Mike on the kitchen table.

And Uncle Mike . . .

According to Mum's last text he knows I'm in some kind of bother. Soon as he finds I'm still not home and reads what I've left for him, he'll mobilise Team Operation Marlin.

Marjory. Starsky. Hutch. Top Cops.

And even if they don't reach me in time, even if I end up like that poor retired security guard, I've left enough clues about Stefan, my sugarcoated evil bastard of a sweet-talking guy, for others to follow my trail.

My trail.

Yeah. Even if Uncle Mike doesn't reach me in time.

And he will. He must. He'd never let me down . . .

Even if Dave Griffen never pulls through to describe who attacked him.

And he will too. He's on the mend. He's strong and super fit . . .

Even if those sirens that seem to be wailing louder by the second are going elsewhere –

But they're not. They're headed this way. They must be. They're clearer. They're blaring. They're outside. Please God. Dear God. I'm sure they are – I might just have cracked Operation Marlin.

Who'd have thought it? Cloddy Quinn doing something useful for once.

Maybe Marjory was right.

I do have the makings of a good cop.

Note to self: I'll look into that if I make it through the next five minutes . . . When Uncle Super Mike arrives. And I get out of here alive . . .

more great stories by

Catherine FORDE

the drowning pond

Hey, guess what?
You're no one. invisible.

But what if one day the glossy
people noticed you,
made you their friend . . .
And then changed their minds?

Say you could get back in by
picking on the weirdo new girl . . .
You would. Wouldn't you?

skarrs

Danny-Boy's got his head shaved for
Grampa Dan's funeral.
Just to see their faces. Is he grieving? Too right.

Instead of sitting in this church, he could be
away in his room.
SKARRS pumping on the speakers.

The way SKARRS play, they could wake the dea

tug of war

When bombs shatter Molly's world,
she's sent to safety in the country
where she lives an idyllic life.

But then it's time to return and she
has to make a heartbreaking choice.